JOYEUX

A MUSKETEER SPACE NOVELLA

TANSY RAYNER ROBERTS

CONTENTS

FOREWORD

In *These Valiant Stars* (Musketeer Space #1) and *A Miracle of Spaceships* (Musketeer Space #2) we meet Dana D'Artagnan, a brash young spaceship pilot who befriends three chaotic Musketeers of the Royal Fleet (Athos, Porthos, Aramis) and swashbuckles her way through a messy web of intergalactic diplomacy, alien war, crashing spaceships and all manner of personal catastrophes.

During her adventures, Dana learns of a series of scandalous events which occurred on Paris Satellite during the festive season of Joyeux, months before she arrived.

This is that Joyeux.

This novella can be experienced before reading the Musketeer Space novels, or afterwards, or (as originally released) in between the two volumes. Choose your own path.

CHAPTER 1
DEVOTIONS
(BRINGING IN THE GREEN)

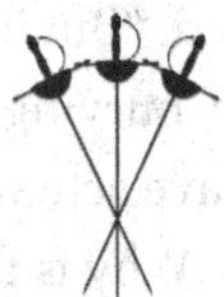

Pollina du Vallon, known to her friends and colleagues as the Musketeer Porthos, awoke in one Musketeer's bed, with another Musketeer sprawled beside her.

For a moment she could not remember the circumstances that had led her here. Aramis, who owned the bed, was nowhere in sight. The Musketeer sleeping beside her was Athos. This was the more immediate concern.

Her head hurt.

Discreetly, without dislodging Athos' arm which was at least partly slung across her hip, Porthos reached down to check whether she was clothed. She found a soft t-shirt and the shorts that she usually wore as underwear, which was a good sign.

"Don't worry," said a low voice beside her. Athos, now awake, was looking at her with amusement in his bright blue eyes. "Your virtue is as intact as ever."

"I wasn't worried," she lied. Then, a moment later. "You're sure?"

He stretched and rolled away from her, taking half the covers with him. "Drink rarely has an effect on my powers of recall. I never forget what happened the night before."

This was new information about her friend, and Porthos stored it away as she did every rare fragment he chose to share. "That must be horrible."

"It's a curse," he agreed. "But in this instance…"

"Ugh." Porthos sat up, burying her head in her hands. "We fly spaceships. We have actual jetpacks, not to mention sobriety patches. Why is there still no real cure for the hangover?"

"Because we're getting old," said Athos unsympathetically. His eyes drifted shut again. He was a more hardened drinker than Porthos and Aramis put together, but he rarely allowed the damage to show. "The important thing here, is that we still haven't lost the bet. Seven days to go."

"The bet?" Porthos had no idea what he was talking about, but then a memory stirred. "Last Joyeux, you mean?" Realisation hit her. "That wench! Did she do this on purpose?"

Athos yawned gently. "She's devious, our Aramis."

Joyeux was a festival of misrule and devotion, of laughter and stupidity and even a little religious contemplation along the way, for those who were into that sort of thing. Last year, on the final night of Joyeux, fuelled by the heady combination of caramel popcorn and tequila shots, Aramis had declared that Athos and Porthos would fuck within a year.

They were both so genuinely horrified by the idea that they pledged fifty credits each against the possibility.

What followed was what Porthos had dubbed 'the shipping war from hell,' in which Aramis spent several months setting up elaborate situations to encourage romance or attraction between her two friends.

It was amusing, then annoying, then funny again, and finally had been all but forgotten. Or so they thought. Porthos sighed. "I thought she'd dropped it."

"On the bright side, it will all be over in seven days," Athos said sleepily. "And we'll have won fifty credits each. So get lost before I succumb to my natural desire to ravish you. I want first shower."

Porthos kicked him as she got out of bed, because she felt like it. She wandered out to Aramis' living space, still in her sleeping shorts as apparently none of them had any shame any more.

The place was a wreck. Like, actually a wreck. The sparse furnishings had been turned over and several chairs were bent and twisted. The comfortable couch had taken some serious damage and what looked like burn from an arc-ray, bursting one arm entirely open. Worst of all, Aramis' books, her precious books of theology, were scattered across the floor as if they had been used as missiles.

"What the actual fuck?" exclaimed Porthos.

Aramis was sprawled out on her couch, naked beneath a sheet. She looked exhausted, and miserable. Her girl-friend Marie Chevreuse was there too, golden and pale against the warmer brown tones of Aramis' skin and hair. Their limbs were tangled together, but they were faced away from each other.

Oh. Now Porthos remembered why she and Athos had retreated to the bedroom. Damn it. Aramis and Chev were fighting again, and from the looks on their faces even in sleep, they were making each other miserable.

Happy bloody Joyeux to everyone.

"Good morning, Captain-Lieutenant Porthos," said the android Bazin, right by her ear. "May your Devotions be deep."

She jumped with surprise. He must have been charging overnight, powered down against the wall while Aramis and Chevreuse tore the apartment and each other apart. "Oh, Bazin. Okay if I help myself to tea?"

There was something about Aramis' devoutly religious engie android that made them all extra polite around him – except Athos who avoided eye contact and stepped around him as if he were a piece of furniture.

A relentlessly pious piece of furniture who was constantly trying to push his pilot out of the Musketeers and into a career in the Church, but furniture nonetheless.

"I will make it for you, Captain-Lieutenant," said the android now, unplugging his connection to the wall. He swiftly overtook Porthos on the way to the kitchen bar. "I have your tea preferences programmed into the food printer."

So much for having something to do with her hands to make this morning less awkward. "Fine," Porthos said, sliding on to the one stool that remained undamaged. "Cheers."

Chevreuse woke up next. "Ugh," she moaned. "What hit me?"

"The apartment, I think," said Porthos with a wave around the wreck of a room.

Chevreuse slid naked out from under the sheet and staggered off in the direction of the bedroom. "Shower. Ugh."

"Athos is in there!" Porthos called after her, but that

was no deterrent. There was a crashing sound from the en suite, as Athos defended his right to not be kicked out of the sonic shower by an equally cranky blonde. It was no contest.

Two minutes later, Athos stormed out wearing nothing but a towel. "Aramis, can we break up with your girlfriend yet? I wish to register some complaints."

"She has a meeting this morning," said Aramis in a low voice. She lay on the couch, her dark eyes alert. "It's stressing her out."

Porthos looked over in surprise – she hadn't even realised that Aramis was awake. "What kind of meeting?"

"With Montbazon. Their marriage contract is nearly up, and they need to make – I don't know. Arrangements. Decisions about the future."

Porthos saw a very specific expression cross Athos' face. It meant: 'how can I steer this conversation away from any reference to feelings and relationships until after I have consumed half my body mass in coffee and hopefully left the apartment altogether?' He used it a lot.

Athos went to the kitchen bar, and Bazin passed him a double espresso without a word.

Porthos still didn't have her cup of tea. If she didn't know better, she might suspect Athos of messing with Bazin's circuitry to prioritise the needs of the hardened coffee drinker. Either that, or the android liked him best, which made no sense at all.

"Will the Captains-Lieutenant be attending church services before the meeting with Amiral Treville?" the android asked politely.

"No," Athos and Porthos muttered in unison.

"Yes," said Aramis automatically. "Wait, what meeting?"

Bazin looked as shifty as was possible for an android with no proper facial expressions. "As requested, all early morning communications were muted because of the late hour at which the Captains-Lieutenant and Minister Chevreuse-Montbazon retired…"

"Unmute," Athos commanded. Alerts chimed from the wrist-studs of all three Musketeers, as well as Aramis' home system. Aramis and Porthos muted theirs again immediately. "An emergency meeting," Athos said as he scanned the notifications. "All Musketeers within the vicinity of Paris Satellite, including those off duty. In twenty minutes."

"No time for church," Aramis said, raising her eyebrows at her android. "Musketeer duty comes first, Bazin, you know that. I'll attend to my soul later."

Chevreuse hurled herself out of the bedroom, now clad in a formal black suit, with pearl studs implanted against the line of her collar bone. Her hair had been combed to a creamy sheen and bleached white to match her pearls. "Here I go. Don't wait up."

"Chev," Aramis said awkwardly.

Her girlfriend leaned in, brushing her lips to Aramis' forehead as if the room around them didn't bear witness to the screaming, damaging fight of the night before. "See you later, babe. We'll talk."

This uptight, professional version of Chevreuse was unsettling. To Porthos' relief, Bazin finally produced a proper cup of tea. It was some consolation for the awkwardness.

To prove she was still the same person despite dressing

like a grown up, Chev openly checked out Athos and his towel before leaving the apartment. "You could do worse, Porthos!" she teased.

Simultaneously, Athos and Porthos flipped their fingers up at her.

In the second before the door zipped shut, they saw Chev falter on her expensive heeled shoes. She screamed "I don't have time for this bullshit," and kept going.

The three Musketeers exchanged glances. Porthos, as the only one of them who was halfway to decently clothed, went to the door and swiped it open. "Whoa."

This was new. New and alarming and probably the reason for the emergency meeting they now had to attend.

Outside Aramis' apartment was a corridor, functional and basic like nearly every other corridor on Paris Satellite. Today, it was covered from floor to ceiling with a bristling green tangle of, well. Leaves. Green creepers, a tangle of ivy and other spiky plants which most definitely did not belong on a space station. Not outside the horticulture banks, anyway.

Athos sucked in a breath, standing close behind Porthos. "What date is it?" he asked.

"The 12th, of course," said Aramis, her dark hair spilling over her shoulders and a sheet vaguely wrapped around her body as she joined them in the doorway. "It's the first day of Joyeux. Devotions."

"Bringing in the green," Athos said in a hiss between his teeth. "Someone's taking the holiday a little too far, and I'm not talking about Joyeux."

"Clothes," Porthos decided, since her friends were too busy staring at the intrusive greenery to think about the important things. "This will be easier to cope with if we're all wearing actual clothes."

Amiral Treville rarely called them all together like this. She preferred to manage the Royal Fleet of Musketeers in twos and threes, which gave her the opportunity to intimidate on a more personal level. This also meant they were less likely to gang up on her, unless the three Musketeers in question were Porthos, Athos and Aramis in which case all bets were off.

There were nearly thirty of them available for this crisis meeting, and Musketeers filled Treville's plexi-glass office. Almost no furniture, as the Amiral spent most of her time on her feet, so they sprawled over each other and the floor like a heap of cats in bright blue flight jackets.

Aramis sat mostly on Porthos, though her feet had found their way to Athos' lap. Being used as furniture on a regular basis was one of those things that went hand in hand with being a friend of Aramis.

Treville was a thick-set, dark-skinned woman in her early fifties, with shoulders so muscled and mighty that she looked like the blueprint for a mecha suit. It was possible that she was less terrifying when her face was not pissed off, but Porthos had worked under her for a long time and could not remember a day when her face looked otherwise.

"This is the situation," Treville rapped out. "Green leaves have been growing out of the walls of the station since 0:00 last night. The labs think it's some kind of nano-virus. The leaves aren't being created out of the molecules of the bloody walls at least, or we'd all be sucking open space right now. A quarter of Paris Satellite has been infested, and we're on track for the whole station to be covered with leaves by the end of the day. What we don't know is why this is happening."

"Obviously it's political," Athos said in the posh drawl he only used around authority figures, or people he wanted to annoy. Which, Porthos had to admit, was most people. "That is to say, religious."

Aramis nudged him in the knee with her boot. "Today is Devotions, Athos. What's that got to do with greenery? There's nothing in the Book of Devotions about eating more salad."

"Wrong religion, sweetness," said Athos with a sharp smile. "The Church of All might pride itself on representing everyone in the solar system, but there's a lot of planetborn citizens that don't feel the same way. The northern hemisphere of Valour has its own celebrations at this time of year."

Porthos frowned. She grew up on Lucretia, one of the orbital cities of the ocean world of Peace, and ran away to Paris Satellite when she was barely of age. She didn't know much about dirtside traditions. "Elementals, you mean?"

Athos' lips were tight beneath the bushy blond beard he had been growing to annoy Amiral Treville. "That's what I mean," he agreed. "Right now, in the northern hemisphere of Valour, the Elemental community are celebrating Winterlight. People cut evergreen boughs and wreaths from the wild and decorate their living quarters with them. It's called bringing in the green. I believe they do something similar on Honour, though their winters aren't nearly as cold."

Porthos glanced around. There were a few nods as some of the other pilots acknowledged what Athos was saying, though most looked as baffled as she felt. The Elemental religion was common for dirtsiders – and was growing in popularity across the planets of Valour and Honour, especially in the countries governed by the New Aristocrats. Since the Regence's marriage to the Prince Consort, it had become almost socially acceptable in some corners to be 'out' as an Elemental, though it was considered rare for them to make a life for themselves in space.

On Paris Satellite it wasn't exactly politic to admit that you were not a follower of the Church of All. The Church was the reason that humanity had survived the expansion of society into space, and would thrive into the future. Even the Prince Consort attended Church of All ceremonies and observed his wife's traditions in public.

Porthos felt an odd, uncomfortable twist in her stomach. She knew Athos had a history back on the planet Valour, and that he came from New Aristocracy. But she had never quite put it together, that he might be an Elemental himself. By the shell-shocked expression on Aramis' face, it had not occurred to her either.

Amiral Treville, who came from a tiny space station so far out that even the tourists refused to bother with it, looked blank. "Why would they do that?" she said finally. "The green. What's the point?"

Athos shrugged. "Why does Repast come before Misrule, why are there seven days of Joyeux? Rituals get repeated because people like repeating rituals. In this case, winters on Valour can be long and cold, and people like a reminder that there's something alive in the world apart from themselves. So, they bring in the green."

"Does the bringing in of the green usually involve nano-viruses?" Treville barked.

Athos laughed at that, a rare and genuine sound from his throat. "Well, no. But Paris is such a forward-thinking city, she does rather love to go one better than everyone else."

The look on Treville's face suggested that she was postponing further interrogation on the subject, not dropping it altogether. She pulled up a pre-determined roster and started calling out assignments. "We're sharing clean up duty with the Red Guard, including Hammers and Sabres. Please do not start any fights, or involve yourself in fights that you will later claim they started. And yes, before any of you whingers speak up, I know that dissolving rogue plants doesn't count as piloting, royal bodyguard work or acts of war. Today's mission is in no way within the remit of the Musketeers. You're still going to pitch in without complaint or I will schedule extra hours in the day specifically to shout at you."

"Stop looking at me like I have two heads," Athos complained to his two friends after they had shuffled out of Treville's office. "You know I'm not religious. Why does it matter which religion I specifically don't bother with?"

Porthos said nothing because he was right, it wasn't important.

"It doesn't matter," said Aramis in a voice which made it clear that yes, it mattered to her. "But you never said."

"I never say anything about anything," Athos sighed. "I'm not even having this conversation with you right now."

"But it's fascinating," Aramis said, squeezing his arm. "We should talk about this. You have a whole different perspective on theology…"

"I have never desired a conversation about theology, Aramis, what makes you think I will start now?"

"It can be my Joyeux present," she said, batting her eyelashes at him.

"No. I'm buying you wine. I always buy you wine. Shut up."

"But – is there a connection between the decoration of Joyeux trees, and the Winterlight tradition of bringing in the green?"

"I would rather *eat* a Joyeux tree than have this conversation with you."

For once, Porthos wished that Treville had given her an assignment as far from Athos and Aramis as possible. She knew why they were so often given shared duty – they worked well as a unit, and for all the trouble they got into as a trio, they got into far worse when they were separated.

Today, there was nothing that could make it worse.

The three of them had been assigned to the Promenade (properly Napoleon Bonaparte Promenade though no one in the Fleet ever called it that because there was a dodgy strip joint near Space Dock B on Lunar Palais that had been known only as *Bonaparte's* for a decade before the Promenade had been given its fancy title and statue).

You couldn't even see the statue when the Musketeers first began work; the Promenade was so choked with holly, ivy and mistletoe sprouting directly out of the walls and ducts. They had sonic disintegrators to deal with the mess, but it was still a slow and methodical grind.

Aramis was trying to prove she wasn't bothered about Athos' refusal to have jolly chats about religious differences by returning to her joke about Athos and Porthos hooking up. It wasn't funny even before she started trying to throw mistletoe at their heads because some idiot had informed her it was connected to a kissing tradition on Valour.

It was even less funny because Aramis, as a born and bred spacer, had no idea what mistletoe even looked like. Porthos was sick of dodging random branches of greenery in the name of mock-romance, and Athos was about ready to punch the next person who asked him to identify which spiky green plant was being shoved in his face.

To make it worse, Captain Claudine Jussac was in command of the Red Hammer unit that had been assigned to this area, and she did everything in her power to irritate all three Musketeers beyond the range of human endeavour.

Before the shift was even half over, Athos and Aramis formulated a complex plan to murder Jussac and dispose of her body without anyone suspecting a thing.

"As the only one of us who can claim the moral high ground of never having shagged her," Porthos snapped at one point. "I reserve the right to wield the spade."

Athos and Aramis exchanged a brief glance. "Fair call," they both agreed.

Porthos never wanted to see another leafy green plant in her life. She didn't care about the difference between holly and mistletoe, she really didn't care whether the trees sticking sideways out of the privacy booths were firs or pines, and if Aramis consulted that *Flora of Valour* app one more time, Porthos was going to break something.

To top it all off, she rounded a corner and found Chef Coquenard picking holly out of an air vent. "Oh," said Porthos, like an idiot. Of course she would run into him when she was scratched up and exhausted and grumpy.

"Pollina," said the large, beautiful man in that deep accent of his that made everything that came out of his mouth sound like a song, or a sultry dessert recipe. "How unexpected. Will we see you at the hotel for Repast this year?"

"I expect so, I'm on Regence duty," Porthos said, trying not to stare at his shoulders. He had really nice shoulders.

Hotel Coquenard was the most exclusive and expensive hotel on Paris Satellite, and they hosted a formal Repast dinner for the royal family every year. Flirting with Chef Coquenard with no intention of ever taking it further was one of Porthos' favourite Joyeux traditions, but they were two days early, and she wasn't properly braced for the impact of that warm smile of his, and her fierce desire to climb him like a tree.

"You're not planning to cook with this, are you?" she managed, reclaiming some of her usual sarcasm as she jabbed a finger at his armful of spiky leaves.

Coquenard laughed, oh God of All, that laugh of his should be illegal. "Table decorations. Why should I not make the most of this unexpected bounty?"

Porthos rolled her eyes. "You realise that these leaves have been created by a possibly malign nano-virus?"

Chef Coquenard blew her a kiss as he carried his armful of holly and ivy away with him. "But it is so lovely to look at," he said. "And style is important."

She stayed standing there for a moment, then shook her head to clear it of the daze that he always inspired in her. She heard a throat clearing nearby and spun around to find Athos looking at her as if she was hilarious.

Porthos glared at him. "If you can hook up with Jussac, of all people, and almost get us killed in the duel that followed your exciting weekend of hate sex, then I can have a crush."

"I didn't say you couldn't have a crush," Athos said mildly. "But I can still find it funny."

"Keep this up, and I'll tell Aramis that I have a crush on *you*."

He raised an eyebrow. "Mutually assured destruction? I don't believe you would do that to either of us."

Damn it, he had called her bluff.

"Don't talk," she huffed. "That not talking thing you do most of the time? Let's have some more of that."

"As you wish, *Pollina*."

By the time their double shift ended, they had cleared the Promenade for business, though much of Paris Satellite was still thick with "festive" greenery.

Aramis headed off to church for Devotions services. She didn't say so to Porthos, but she obviously had plans to meet with Chevreuse after that. Athos disappeared without a word, which meant he wanted to drink alone. Any attempt to inflict friendly company on him would be met with his impersonation of an emotionally-repressed statue, and Porthos was too tired to be bothered.

She shared a meal with her engie Bonnie, and collapsed in bed some time around 22:00.

She was awoken by her comm chiming, a few minutes after midnight. It was a text message from Athos, and it took her a moment to focus on the glowing words along her wrist before she could read them properly.

LOOK OUTSIDE YOUR DOOR.

When Porthos had arrived home to her apartment a few hours earlier, the greenery was so thick in the corridor that she had used her pilot's slice to free the main entry from weeds and tangled vine. That explained the dream she half-remembered, of being smothered by trees and flowers.

Now, as she padded barefoot to the door and swiped it open, there was no green.

The corridor was clean and empty, as if the leaves had never been there. There was, however, an odd kind of feeling as if the whole of Paris Satellite was breathing more easily than before. Porthos could smell the green on the air, though there was no trace of it left.

It made her smile.

MERRY WINTERLIGHT, she texted back to Athos, before returning to her bed.

He replied a moment later. HAPPY FUCKING JOYEUX.

This time, when Porthos slept, she dreamed of flight and stars and all the usual shit. So that was all right.

CHAPTER 2
RESTRAINT
(THE BURYING OF PAST SINS)

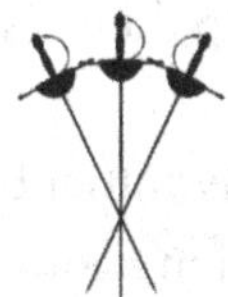

Athos (who was not now, nor ever would be again Olivier Armand d'Autevielle, the Comte de la Fere) had not slept.

This was not unusual. The trick was to make sure that neither Porthos nor Aramis figured it out. They spent far too much of their energy worrying about him, and he employed regular damage control to keep their concern at a level he could tolerate.

Coffee helped. Especially on an early shift like today, where the three of them sat at a cafe table in the middle of the Stellar Concourse, surrounded by people and noise and colour and all those other symptoms of human society.

His reputation for being an unsociable bastard who was grumpy at the best of times was also on his side.

"How was Chevreuse last night?" Porthos asked. She had ordered tea and a plate of fruit and pastries, occasionally pushing a morsel in Athos' direction. "After the meeting?"

"Quiet," said Aramis, who had water and plain rice cakes in front of her. She took the traditional fast of Restraint more seriously than anyone Athos knew. At least she had stopped sending him the reproachful little 'why won't you discuss religious contrast theory with me' digs that made yesterday *so* much fun. "I don't think she and Montbazon have made up their mind if they're going to renew the contract."

Athos would generally rather bite his own arm off than contribute to a conversation about anyone's marriage, but that detail caught his attention. "Is Chev planning to quit her job at the Palace?"

Aramis' girlfriend was the Minister of Royal PR, and she was as deeply passionate about her work as she was about the constant opportunity to make life difficult for Cardinal Richelieu. It was the latter personality quirk that made Chevreuse an honorary Musketeer as far as Athos was concerned, though she was almost as irritating in all other respects as his two friends.

"Of course not," said Aramis, too quickly.

"Only married or church-sworn citizens are allowed to work at the Palace," Porthos said, picking up on Athos' train of thought. The morality clause was one of the stupidest technicalities around, but there was no denying the power it held in and around Paris Satellite and Lunar Palais. "So why wouldn't she… oh."

"Oh," Aramis agreed. "She has to be married to keep her job, and her husband has no objection to extending their marriage contract for another term. But Chevreuse has implied that her decision is something that – I should have an opinion about."

Porthos tried to hide her smile, but caught Athos' expression at the last moment and collapsed into laughter.

"Pol!" Aramis wailed. "Some sympathy please."

"I'm sorry, love," said Porthos, snuffling into her hand. "But I thought the whole point of you shagging married women all over the city was so you didn't end up in this situation. Is Chev expecting you to propose?"

Aramis buried her head in her hands, and it was only Athos' quick work that saved her water glass from falling off the table. "I don't know," she whined. "She hasn't said it outright."

"Ah," Athos nodded. Part of the reason he and Chevreuse got along so well was that they shared the preference to not discuss personal matters out loud. If only it had rubbed off on these two, his life would be closer to perfect than he had ever deserved. "Explains the yelling and throwing things."

"I think we're either breaking up or getting married," Aramis moaned. "And we're not getting married. So…"

Athos tried to discreetly print another coffee without Porthos realising how quickly he had choked down the last one. When he glanced up from the table controls, her dark eyes caught his.

"Athos, have you slept recently?"

"Sleep is very important," he said solemnly. "Seven hours a night is highly recommended."

"That's not an answer."

"I've been thinking about Winterlight," he went on, to change the subject.

"The leaves sorted themselves out," said Aramis. "Didn't they? Whatever prank someone decided to pull is – well, it's done."

"There are seven days of Joyeux, and nineteen days of Winterlight," said Athos. "If a point is being made with this festive terrorism, then they're not going to stop at one incident."

"Oh," said Porthos, letting the sleep issue drop. "Festive terrorism?"

"Direct quote from Treville. She called me this morning to get a briefing on Elemental traditions for Winterlight."

"Really, nineteen days?" Aramis broke in. "Isn't that excessively religious?"

"That's rich, coming from you," Athos shot back.

"What's today?" Porthos asked. There was a look on her face that Athos didn't like, and it had nothing to do with work. It was her 'uh-oh something is wrong with Athos' expression, and if he didn't nip it in the bud he faced terrible consequences. Like, having to drink less for a few weeks to prove he was okay. He hated that.

"Today," said Athos, not letting his face even twitch to show Porthos that he was on to her being on to him. "In Winterlight terms, is the burying of past sins."

"Huh," said Aramis. "I suppose that's a lot like Restraint, really, isn't it?"

"Depends on how deeply you bury those sins," said Porthos. "What did Treville say when you told her?"

Athos sipped his second coffee. It went down more smoothly than the first. "She hoped we weren't going to end up with a space station full of dirt."

Amiral Treville was driving her Musketeers around the bend. They had been hauled off most of their regular duties in order to patrol and investigate any areas of Paris Satellite that their commander felt were potential targets for the festive terrorists.

Given how little they had to go on, 'potential targets' meant locations associated with Joyeux celebrations, rituals or displays. Athos had heard so many Joyeux carols in the last three hours that he was about to strangle the next choirmaster with a green sparkly ribbon, and he had nearly got into several fights with Red Hammers because of crossing Church territory.

The fight he hadn't been able to avoid involved a down and dirty sword duel behind a choir stand, and tinsel. He didn't want to talk about it.

Transporting three rowdy fleur-de-lis players from the palace to their practice tanks on Paris Satellite wasn't the kind of duty that Athos usually looked forward to, but right now he was relieved to be away from the singing and the sparkly lights and the belligerent Red Hammers for a couple of hours.

Prince Alek, already geared up in his TeamJoust armour, was the first through the hatchway of Athos' ship, the *Parry Riposte*. "We got the sulky one!" he cheered, and stretched his arms back behind him. "You owe me ten, Conrad."

Conrad Su, the Prince Consort's tailor and teammate, swiped his wrist stud against the prince's so that credit could be exchanged between them. "Don't spend it all at once," he teased in return.

The two of them looked like brothers, with the same gold-tan skin and metallic scale pattern down the side of their faces that marked them out as being from Auster, one of the many uncomfortably hot continents of the planet

Honour. Alek was taller, with his hair dyed ruby red, and Conrad shorter with silver highlights in his natural black hair.

Their third teammate piled in after them, dragging a visitor by the hand. "Hello, Athos," said Chev with a grin, clasping his arm briefly. "Long time, no see."

Her affair with Aramis was secret, of course, thanks to that precious morality clause in the Palace contracts. Only their close friends knew about it, and Athos didn't know if close friends included her fellow Emerald Knights.

"Minister Chevreuse," Athos said formally.

She screwed up her face at him. "Don't do that, that's – ugh. Politeness does not suit you at all. This is Buck, by the way. She's coming to watch our practice."

Athos hesitated only a moment. The woman beside Chevreuse was a duchess, and the ambassador of Valour. Her presence here on Luna Palais had been tabloid fodder for the last month. "Your grace," he said, with a bow of his head, because there were some formalities drilled into him so deep that he was never getting rid of them.

"None of that for me either, Captain," said the Duchess of Buckingham with a wide grin. "Call me Buck." She wore cargo pants and a tank top, reddish copper curls hanging long and unfettered around her shoulders. Athos guided her in the direction of the aft seats, well away from the many cables of his helm and harness. Just because he wore his hair and beard too long for strict safety protocols didn't mean he was going to let a peer of Valour take the same risk.

Buck was followed by an unassuming looking fellow who introduced himself as "Linton Gray, her grace's aide."

Athos shook his hand, and the aide gave him a faintly startled look as if he hadn't expected that level of courtesy.

"Ignore him, I'm off duty, don't even let him on the ship!" Buck called, but she was laughing.

Mr Gray looked exasperated. He chose a seat on the side wall of the cockpit. He arranged his harness with practiced hands, waving away Athos' attempts to help, and read quietly from a tablet as they prepared for take off. His hands shook a little, which suggested he was not comfortable with space travel. Athos sympathised with the man's 'don't look at me, I don't want to be here,' vibe, and respected that by ignoring him entirely.

Chev slid into the seat beside Athos, her game armour creaking. Her hair was bright violet today. She liked to match hair colour to duty – auburn or brown for official Ministerial duties, her natural blonde for when she wanted to relax, and something ridiculous when playing fleur-de-lis.

He had never known until yesterday that she preferred pearl-white when holding official meetings with her husband, but the number of times Athos had seen Chevreuse with her husband could be counted on one hand. Montbazon was not a clingy spouse.

"The seasonal greenery disappeared as quickly as it arrived," she said as Athos strapped himself into his own helm and harness, activating the connections that he usually had his engie Grimaud to help him with – she was off on leave visiting her family for the season. "Any leads?"

"Treville suspects Joyeux elves," said Athos, deadpan.

Chevreuse threw back her head and laughed. "Oh, elves. You can take elves."

"With one hand tied behind my back," he agreed, and let his mind fall forward into his ship. This, at least, was something he could control.

Back on Paris Satellite, Athos escorted his party of VIP players to the zero-gravity practice tank and waited until the relief protective detail arrived: Aramis with Cadet Fontaine, one of the new recruits.

"You're off duty now?" Aramis asked, her eyes drawn to the scene beyond the plexi-glass wall of the zero gravity tank. The Duchess of Buckingham was an experienced fleur-de-lis player herself, and had joined the three team-mates in the tank as they ran through their practice moves.

Mr Linton Gray, who was no more fond of sport than he was of spaceships, read from his tablet and occasionally glanced up to check that all was well with Buck. Athos liked the fact that the other man had not attempted to make conversation with him.

A couple of engies in the control booth managed the gravity settings and responded to requests from the play-ers, throwing up holographic recordings of particular moves or former games to aid the exercises. Large latte cups balanced awkwardly on the desk in the booth, almost as big as the engies' heads.

Coffee, now there was an idea. Or better yet, wine. Athos was an expert in burying his own past sins and sorrows, but he much preferred to drown them.

"If Treville hasn't cancelled all downtime to hunt for elves and mistletoe," he said in response to Aramis' question.

"Not yet. Grab a nap while you can." Aramis pulled her gaze away from her girlfriend to look seriously at Athos for a moment, her hand brushing his sleeve. "Really, darling. You can't run on no sleep. We do notice. Brandy isn't a substitute for occasional unconsciousness."

Athos knocked his knuckles gently against her shoulder. "Stop noticing. I'm fine."

As he left, Mr Gray raised his head for a moment and gave him a polite nod. Unsettled, Athos returned it.

He was fine, of course he was fine. That was why he headed straight for the nearest bar. It was an obviously terrible bar, from the decor. 'Never trust a bar with mirrors on its walls,' Porthos always said, and this one had reflective surfaces everywhere, even on the ceiling. Athos' own pallid face stared back at him from every corner.

No wonder Aramis was concerned. Athos looked terrible.

Even for mid-shift, it was surprisingly empty for a bar so close to the entertainment hubs, but as the bartender came over to take his order, Athos remembered that this was Restraint, the second day of Joyeux. The more devout half of the station's residents were fasting for the next eight hours. No stimulants, no protein. Rice cakes and water and nothing more, to cleanse their souls before tomorrow's day of feasting and merriment.

Far more Paris residents would take part in tomorrow's traditions than today's, but that didn't mean the rest wouldn't be discreet about continuing to indulge their vices. There was no reason for him to hesitate. Joyeux was not his holiday, and Athos could all but taste the drink he really wanted.

Back home on Castellion, a continent of the planet Valour that had no hold over Athos whatsoever (not any more), most people were not celebrating Joyeux, but Winterlight. The burying of past sins. Ever since he had said that aloud, Athos had been thinking of his own sins, the ones that he had buried long ago. Today they felt far from buried. They bubbled constantly away at him, just beneath his skin.

He wanted brandy, or whiskey, or wine, anything that would let him sleep. But if he slept he would dream, and after spending the morning pushing away bad memories, he knew who he would see in his dreams.

Anything but that.

"Espresso," he said instead. "Double shot," and gripped the edge of the bar until the bartender brought him a freshly printed cup of heat and blackness that would let him stay awake a little longer.

We bury them beneath the earth, and forgive ourselves the wrongs we did to them in life, so that life itself may continue. It was an old family prayer, and absolutely the last thing he needed in his head right now.

Athos knocked back the coffee, and felt instantly sick. He should eat something. When had he last eaten?

His hand shook as he lowered the cup. Perhaps he would order that brandy after all, to keep himself on an even measure until this day was over and he could breathe again.

"Hello, Olivier," said a voice so soft that he thought at first it was entirely in his head.

Of course it was in his head. How could it be otherwise? And yet, when Athos whirled around, he saw sharp cheekbones and pale grey eyes behind a soft fall of metallic silver hair. That smile, oh God and hell and everything in between, that smile.

He saw his husband, and it shattered something inside him.

Aramis had left her old name behind long ago: it no longer said anything about her. She had no need to be anyone but Aramis: no past and no regrets.

No old regrets, at least. She was racking up new ones at a pretty high pace these days. Some of them were even about things that had not happened yet, but were inevitable.

Like breaking her own heart.

Aramis loved to watch Chevreuse in the air. There was a carelessness about her in the zero-gravity tank that she never achieved anywhere else, except perhaps in bed with her back arched up and her head thrown back, a moan upon her lips.

The trouble with being in love with a devastatingly intelligent woman was that her brain was always firing, working on five different problems at once. Chev was wickedly funny and smart and sharp in several different ways, and yet there was always a part of her that was at work, even when she was supposed to be at play.

In the tank, Chevreuse and Alek and Conrad were beautiful together, responding physically to each other's cues: a dance of accuracy and strength and teamwork. The

Emerald Knights. Aramis had been a fan of the team even before she started sleeping with one of them.

Putting the Prince Consort in this team with two people he could deeply trust was the best piece of PR that Chevreuse had ever built for the royal family. The Regence gained ten popularity points almost overnight, the first time that the Emerald Knights played a full game.

And Prince Alek, who always tried to make the best of things despite having so few friends and allies in a Palace that never forgot he was an Elemental dirtsider from Honour… in the tank, he was happy.

Today, something different was going on. The inclusion of the Valour Ambassador should have made things awkward, but Buck was a cheery bundle of energy and the other three fed off that. Effortlessly, a team of three had become a team of four, and there was a beautiful symmetry to them.

Too bad that no one had ever heard of a four person Zero Gravity TeamJoust league.

They separated into pairs, Chev and Conrad working on a complex pole pass they had been trying to perfect all season, while Alek and Buck dared each other to race up the walls, skimming the almost invisible hand-hold loops that were fitted against the plexi-glass. Neck and neck, they tossed laughing looks at each other.

"They're hot together," said young Fontaine with a cheeky grin.

"Yes," Aramis said without thinking, and then realised what that unsettling feeling was in her stomach. The Prince and the Duchess were flirting. Really flirting, with every inch of their ridiculously fit and muscular bodies.

She glanced over at Mr Linton Gray, who met her eyes

briefly and then turned his eyes back to his tablet, making it clear that there was nothing that he wished to discuss.

It wasn't like Aramis could throw stones when it came to adultery, but this was the Prince freaking Consort. A flirtation between Alek and Buck meant trouble. She'd have to have a word with Chev, see if she had noticed the danger signs.

Except, of course she had. As Aramis watched, her girlfriend pushed herself between the Prince and the Duchess with a teasing laugh, pulling Alek into the centre of the tank with her. Conrad matched Buck with a grin that was all challenge, and in the next moment it was the two of them skimming the edge of the tank, while Alek and Chevreuse ran through a drill for airspins.

Aramis relaxed. Chevreuse was on top of it. There was no way Prince Alek would have an affair that brought down the government, not on Chev's watch.

It was going to hurt, breaking up with this brilliant, gorgeous woman. It hurt already. But Aramis couldn't see any other future for them.

Her comm stud trilled with the specific tone that meant Porthos was calling. Aramis raised her wrist to her mouth. "What's up?"

"It's in the coffee," said Porthos, sounding rattled. More than rattled. "Have you had any coffee today?"

"It's Restraint," Aramis said more sharply than she should. "I'm fasting."

"I know, but have you?"

"No."

"Ask the kid too."

"Fontaine," Aramis said, raising her voice a little. "Have you drunk coffee today?"

The recruit looked confused. "I had a dandelion tea with breakfast? Before, um, I remembered about the fast."

"What's going on?" Aramis asked her friend.

"It's in the fucking coffee," Porthos snarled. "The burying of past sins? Festive terrorism via nano-virus? Today's little present is in the coffee."

"Oh," said Aramis, as this sank in. "Bloody hell."

"You need multiple doses before it kicks in, so the incidents didn't make an obvious pattern before now, but it's been building across the station all day. The victims are suffering hallucinations, all related to things they feel guilty about in their pasts. The hospice beds are filling, and there's no bloody cure yet. We can only hope it wears off at midnight like the last one. Happy fucking Joyeux."

"Athos," Aramis blurted out. "Is he –" God of All. If ever there was a caffeine addict with a haunted past, it was Athos.

Mr Gray had set his tablet down, was watching her with open curiosity. Aramis tried to keep her fear off her face.

"He tried to throw himself off the balcony overlooking Charlemagne Boulevard," said Porthos, her voice cracking. "Took three Red Hammers to hold him back. Never thought I'd have a reason to be grateful to those bastards."

Aramis sank into the seat below her. "He's okay?"

"No, he's not okay," Porthos hissed. "Did you know he was married once? He's at the hospice now, in an actual padded cell because the medics aren't willing to knock him out until they are sure how the drugs will respond to the nano-virus."

"Married," Aramis whispered. She had never known Athos to have a relationship longer than three days, which was for the best considering his appalling taste in partners. "What has that got to do with…"

"He keeps raving about a husband, a dead husband who is apparently *talking to him right now* about how they murdered each other. It's bad, Aramis. I can't —" Porthos paused, her words breaking up for a moment with a snuffling sound. "Sorry. I know you can't come. There's no way we'd be able to find another Musketeer to cover your detail, not with more of these incidents springing up everywhere. Just make sure no one gives the Prince Consort a cappuccino while he's on station, okay? The food printers across Paris have had their caffeine options deactivated now, so we can only hope it doesn't get worse before it gets better."

"Got it," said Aramis, her chest tight. She needed to be with Porthos and Athos right now, not babysitting a bunch of jousters who were perfectly capable of taking care of themselves. "Keep in touch about our boy."

"Of course."

Linton Gray was still watching her, his eyes calm and steady. "Trouble?" he asked.

Aramis nodded tightly. "Don't drink any coffee," she managed, not trusting herself to say more than that.

It was hard to watch the rest of the practice, knowing that disaster was breaking out across Paris, and Athos… what the hell was going on with Athos? Aramis couldn't even look at the tank, too busy worrying about what was going on back at the hospice.

"Captain Aramis?" spoke up Fontaine, sounding nervous. "Is that something we should be worried about?"

At first, Aramis wasn't sure what the cadet meant, but then she saw that the two engies in the control booth were having some kind of fight. One of them lunged forward, and the other grabbed her. A cup fell to the floor in the scuffle and Aramis felt as if she had been punched. *It's in the coffee.*

"Break it up," she yelled at Fontaine and ran forward, waving at the tank in the hopes of getting their attention. Conrad noticed her first. He had always been a bright boy. He reached out and said something to Buck. They both stopped climbing, hanging on with hands and feet to the wall loops.

Conrad tipped his head back, yelling a command to Chevreuse and Alek.

If they only played Cinquefoil, all of them would be equipped with jet packs that introduced greater thrust (and violence) in the gameplay. But this was fleur-de-lis, and the only thrust they were allowed came from basic physics.

Alek and Chevreuse had miniature thrusters on their belts for safety protocols, but they were still in the centre of the tank and moving too damned slowly.

Aramis leaped over the seats and ran to the control booth, where Fontaine had already reached the tussling engies with Linton Gray hot on her heels. It was going to be fine. There were so many layers of safety built into the damned computers, it wasn't like anything bad could really happen, they were preparing for the possibility, that was all…

Seconds before she reached the control booth, Aramis turned her head back, and so she saw the moment when the zero gravity failed. She saw the Prince Consort smacking into the plexi-glass wall because Chevreuse had fucking well shoved him in that direction, the last breath of zero gravity pushing her back, out of reach of safety.

As Aramis tripped over the last seat and fell in a heap on the hard metal floor, she saw the woman she loved fall from mid air to land in a crumpled heap on the base of the tank.

Someone screamed in horror and she only realised after the fact that it must have been her.

Athos did not usually look this tidy when he slept. Usually he was a crumpled heap of limbs and hair, after fighting the darkness to the last second. Now, he lay perfectly straight in the bed of the private room in the hospice, his face wiped of his usual layers of sarcasm, defensiveness and manic energy.

Aramis reached out and touched his ridiculous shoulder-length blond hair with her fingertips. Even his beard looked neater than usual. So strange.

"He'll never forgive you if you shave his head while he's out of it," remarked Porthos from the chair on the other side of their partner. She was knitting. Porthos knitted when she was stressed, working continually on a garment that was vaguely polygonal and had far too many dropped stitches to ever be salvageable.

"Might be worth it," said Aramis, tugging at Athos' hair lightly, not enough to stir him. "One of these days, this hair is going to be the death of him."

"Thought he was going to be the death of me today," whispered Porthos.

Losing Athos was the thing they both feared the most.

He was the vulnerable one, the one with cracks running through him. Keeping him in one piece had become their joint mission, since the day they first took responsibility for him on a mountainside on Valour.

Grimaud helped to a point, though there were times when Aramis thought that Athos' engineer hated him as much as she loved him like a son. The same could be said for Treville, who had a stupidly soft spot for Athos but expressed it mostly through shouting.

It was ridiculous that they needed so many people to keep one man on his feet and functioning. But he was worth the trouble, most days.

From what the medics had gleaned from other victims of the coffee virus, this particular piece of nastiness ran its course after a couple of hours. Athos was clear of it already, but the drugs that the medics had pumped into him should keep him unconscious for the remainder of the late shift.

Aramis couldn't find it in her to be sorry. It must be the best sleep he had had in months. "The other victims didn't remember what they saw when the virus was active," she said quietly.

"I know," Porthos sighed.

"So are you going to tell him? That we've unlocked his tragic backstory?" Aramis hadn't witnessed Athos' ranting phase, but Porthos had given her the gist – Athos had been married, actually married, back in that fancy life he lived before his two best friends rescued him and brought him to Paris to be a Musketeer. He held himself accountable for his husband's death. And more – there had to be more to it than that. Aramis burned to know everything.

Porthos put her knitting aside now, fury spilling over

into her voice. "Should I rub it in that he confessed all his dark secrets when he was out of his mind, things he obviously never wanted to share with us? Of course not. He'd never forgive us for knowing."

Aramis nodded, her hands tugging at the neat bedspread that someone had folded around Athos as if he was an old fashioned letter in a paper envelope. "There might be a time when he needs us to know."

"Oh yes," Porthos said sarcastically. "And on that day – I'm sure Athos will talk to us openly about his feelings."

Neither of them laughed.

"Go back to Chevreuse," Porthos said after a long silence between them. "I'll stay with our broken soldier for a bit longer."

Aramis did not want to go, but Porthos was right. The level below was in chaos — Aramis had slipped out when Amiral Treville thundered through the hospice to take charge of the situation. But she should get back there to help sort it all out.

After leaving a soft kiss on Athos' forehead and another for Porthos who probably needed it more, Aramis returned downstairs to see whether things had settled down.

Far from it. The floor had been cleared of all non-essential medical personnel but now Cardinal Richelieu of all people had arrived to escort the Prince Consort and Ambassador Buckingham to Lunar Palais.

Alek finally agreed to leave under protest, looking back reluctantly at the room where Chevreuse was still being treated. "Stay, Conrad," he ordered his teammate. "Let me know how she is. Any time of night."

"Of course Mr Su will not disturb the Regence's sleep

or your own with medical information that could be easily shared over breakfast," the Cardinal said smoothly, extending her arm to guide Buck along the corridor and away. Mr Linton Gray followed Buck like the shadow he was.

Aramis was able to slide past them, mostly unnoticed, though Prince Alek caught her eye for a moment and gave her an awkward smile. Aramis and Chevreuse had never been as open about their relationship in front of Chev's people as they were with Aramis' friends, but she thought Alek knew the score.

Conrad Su certainly did. He was relieved when Aramis joined him, even giving her half of a hug around her shoulders. "Chev woke up a few minutes ago," he told her.

"Oh," said Aramis, wincing. "How'd that go for everyone?"

"She threw a medical trolley at the crew who were working on her leg. It mostly didn't hit them."

"That's something."

Aramis had waited around long enough earlier to over-hear the diagnosis, before she went to check on her friends. Chevreuse was going to be all right – no lasting damage – and the safety protocols built into the tank had at least partly cushioned her fall. But she had landed with one leg folded under her, and the bone had smashed in twelve places.

Most of her injuries could be mended within 24 hours, but the thorough nature of the damage meant that the ankle was going to take four days.

The Emerald Knights' final game of the season was two days away. Even if Chevreuse could play with a partially shattered ankle – which was debatable – she had at least three proscribed medications running in her veins right now, and it was illegal to play within 48 hours of major medipatch treatment.

All of which meant that Chevreuse had awoken from her brief medical coma to be informed that her injuries (and more importantly, her treatment) rendered her ineligible to play on Misrule.

It wasn't a surprise to Aramis that her temperamental girlfriend was not taking the news well. "Has – uh, anyone informed Montbazon? That his wife's in the hospice?"

"He sent flowers," said Conrad with a roll of his eyes.

"Classy."

A harried looking medic came out and looked from Conrad to Aramis. "Friends of the patient? We've given her some sedatives to calm her down. I'm almost sure she won't assault either of you if you choose to go in, but one at a time, please."

Conrad stepped back so quickly that it made Aramis dizzy. "You're up, Captain."

"Thanks," Aramis said dryly.

Chevreuse looked terrible. Her complexion was pale and she seemed exhausted, like she had been fighting a mecha bare-handed.

Aramis was almost afraid to touch her, but she leaned in bravely and gave her a kiss on the forehead. She settled back into the visitor's chair, keeping a healthy distance between them. "How are you doing?"

"Coming to terms with the fact that we just lost our

chance at a perfect, unbeaten season two days before the last game," Chevreuse complained. "The painkillers and medipatches are taking care of all the broken bits. Bastard things."

"It wasn't reasonable to expect the medics to hold off on putting you back together until after the game," Aramis said softly.

"I know. Shut up." Chevreuse closed her eyes. "I want to scream and hit things, but I think they've given me anti-violence drugs. I'm going all floaty and accepting."

"Thank goodness for anti-violence drugs. Glad they invented those."

There was a long pause, and just when Aramis began to wonder if Chevreuse had fallen asleep, she spoke again. "Now you get to say I told you so."

"What? Why would I do that?"

"If we were all as devout about observing Restraint as you, coffee sales for today would have been nil, and no one would have gone crazy and had punch-ups near gravity controls."

Aramis was insulted that Chevreuse thought she would even think such a thing, let alone say it. "I don't expect anyone else to share my…" There was no way to describe her feelings about religion without sounding preachy. "I wouldn't."

"You know what's funny? I actually did observe the fast today." Chevreuse let her face curve back into a smile. "Ironic."

That was a surprise. Chevreuse was as publicly devout as she needed to be for her political position, but she never let belief or ritual affect her daily life. "Why?" Aramis asked.

"Peace offering for you. Not that you noticed, you bitch. And I thought – we've got a big game coming up. Could do with a few godly points up my sleeve." Chevreuse laughed slowly, and then winced as the anti-pain drugs failed to do their job for a brief moment. "Told you it was funny."

Aramis let out a long, shaky breath. "You scared the hell out of me today."

"I know," muttered her girlfriend. "Didn't mean to. Should have known how you'd react."

"What?" Were they talking about the same thing?

"Seemed good manners, that's all."

"Saving the Prince Consort and falling twenty feet directly on to your ankle?"

The balcony overlooking Charlemagne Boulevard was at least thirty feet up. Would Athos have gotten away with a four day hospice visit and a busted ankle? Aramis couldn't stop thinking about it. What had Porthos left out of the story? What could be so bad about her friend's secret past marriage that he wanted to throw himself off a bloody balcony?

"No, dimwit. Asking what you thought about renewing the marriage contract with Montbazon."

Oh, that. Aramis winced. Chevreuse was high on pain relief and she wanted to talk about their relationship. This wouldn't end well. "We don't have to —"

Chevreuse's eyes flew open suddenly. They were bright purple to match her hair. She liked to switch out lenses to suit her mood or her fashion choices. "Didn't mean to pressure you."

"It's fine," Aramis said, annoyed now.

"Didn't ask you to marry me."

"I know."

"S'the trouble with infidelity," Chevreuse sighed. Her body relaxed into the sigh as if the drugs were kicking in more effectively. So that was good. "Doesn't come with a renewal clause or a contract. Renegotiation. Cooling off period. You sort of have to – feel your way through it, until…"

"Until what?" Aramis couldn't help asking.

"Until it ends."

That stung, but not as much as it should have done. "I'll come by tomorrow," Aramis promised, and kissed Chevreuse on the mouth this time. "We can talk then. It's okay, love."

"Should have stayed friends with you, from the start," Chevreuse whispered, her eyes well and truly closed now. "The Musketeer Aramis never lets go of her friends."

Aramis stayed by Chevreuse's bedside, long after she was asleep.

Of all the breakups in her life thus far, this was her least favourite.

CHAPTER 3
REPAST

(AND THE RAINS FALL)

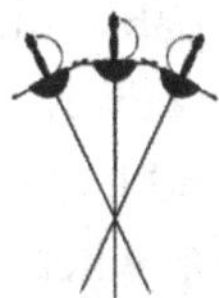

ENTREE: BATTERED CHEVREUSE WITH SCRAMBLED ATHOS ON TOAST.

thos' beard itched. For the first time in the six months since he had started growing it out, he felt the urge to shave the bloody thing back to the light skim of stubble it used to be. His hair, too. It had started as a joke to tease Amiral Treville after she mocked him for his New Aristocrat airs and graces, and turned into a colossal game of chicken whereby Treville pretended not to notice it was there, and Athos pretended that he hadn't done such a childish thing to annoy his boss.

They were at stalemate.

The long hair and beard had another purpose. Ever since Athos joined the Musketeers, most of the pilots in the fleet had regarded him warily – even when he looked exactly like the rest of them, basic buzz cut all over, he carried himself differently and nothing could be done about the accent that marked him out as someone who belonged in a planetary parliament rather than a cockpit. His peers were suspicious of who this New Aristocrat had been before he donned the flight jacket.

The only ones who weren't wary of him were Porthos and Aramis, who accepted him as a brother and an equal. Athos had not intended to find friends on Paris Satellite. He had been searching for absolution and the distraction of steady work, not a new family.

So he kept the beard and let his hair grow out. Played the mischievous, manic fop when he was in a good mood, and the surly drunk when he was not. Gave them all as many excuses as they needed for the odd looks and the suspicious smiles. Meanwhile, Porthos rolled her eyes and complained about health and safety as his hair inched longer and longer. Aramis occasionally threatened to shave him in his sleep.

This was something he could control.

Today was not a good day. If Athos could stop his hands shaking, he would shave himself raw, scalp and jaw alike.

Instead, he sat in an uncomfortable metal chair in the corner of Minister Marie Chevreuse-Montbazon's room in the hospice, thinking about the time that he fell asleep in Aramis' apartment and woke up to discover that Chev had used her colour wand to paint his beard in rainbow stripes.

She looked different in sleep – washed out in this room with no colour. Even her purple hair only made the rest of her look paler and more sickly. She could do with a few rainbow stripes of her own. Finally, she grumbled herself awake.

Athos raised a hand in greeting, noting that his fingers

barely trembled. That was an improvement on an hour ago. "Morning, ma'am."

"Ugh," the Royal Minister of PR muttered, cracking her jaw. "Why are you here? Of all people to be faced with first thing in the morning, *you*."

"They won't let me discharge myself."

"You look terrible," she said, regarding him critically as she struggled into a sitting position.

"Right back at you, sweetness." It was a relief to be around Chevreuse, to be treated with her usual brand of half-hearted disdain. Better than the kicked puppy expression he had seen on Porthos' face, when he first woke up from the haze.

"Oh, of course," Chev said, flopping back on her pillows. "It was in the coffee this time, wasn't it? No wonder it got you."

"Not as badly as it got you," Athos said, and flipped up the other end of her sheet to reveal the plastic medi-cast wrapped around her lower leg.

Chevreuse looked at it for a long moment. "Fuck."

"Perhaps it's the universe's way of telling you that there's no such thing as a perfect season," Athos suggested. Even as he said it, he knew that was too far.

She glared at him through narrowed eyes. "The game's not until tomorrow. I have time to come up with a plan."

"Seriously? Your ankle won't be fully mended by the game, and even if they let you play on it – which they won't – medi-intervention within 48 hours automatically disqualifies you."

"I know," Chevreuse said with an airy wave. "Mere details. Is my clamshell around?"

Athos investigated the cupboard at the back of the

room and found her belongings, including a bright green clamshell tablet which he passed to her.

"We've got three possible reserve players to choose from, so the Emerald Knights can still win the cup," she muttered, calling up several windows of information at once. "But for the perfect season, it has to be *us*, the same players. We won fifteen games in a row, and now we're going to lose the record on a technicality? It's not bloody fair."

The holographic head of Chevreuse's assistant Rohan popped suddenly up out of the tablet. "Minister, I didn't expect to hear from you today. We've cleared your calendar... how are you feeling?"

"I'm fucking terrific, Rohan, what do you mean you cleared my calendar? I'm expected at the Royal Repast at the Hotel Coquenard for luncheon, and I will accompany their highnesses and the Valour Ambassador to their various appearances across Paris this afternoon, before returning to Lunar Palais for the ceremonial supper at the Palace."

"I was given to understand that you should not be on your feet for several days, Minister," said Rohan apologetically. "You have been awarded sick leave until the end of Joyeux..."

"What?" Chevreuse snapped. "I can't have a holiday in the middle of a holiday, this is when I have the most work to do! Unclear my calendar right now, or I will visit your family home and burn all the presents." She slammed the clamshell shut. "Athos, weren't you supposed to be on Repast duty?"

Athos nodded. "I was, with Aramis and Porthos, but Treville forced me to take 24 hours of leave thanks to the coffee incident." He only had jumbled, dreamlike images of what had happened during the hours he was overtaken by the nano-virus. He could have gone to work today like nothing had happened, he was sure of it.

But when he woke up in the middle of the night, he had found Porthos watching over him like he was a baby lamb. She kept lurching in his direction as if she wanted to hug him, but was afraid he might be bruised by her touch. When Aramis brought him breakfast, she all but avoided eye contact. Both of them had refused to support Athos when Amiral Treville marched into his hospice room after breakfast and announced his enforced leave.

Treville hadn't yelled at him. That was the worst of it. She allowed him to negotiate 24 hours of leave down from her initial offer of a month, and walked away leaving Athos feeling that he had been tricked into something.

Porthos and Aramis and maybe even Treville knew something that he didn't, and he was almost afraid to find out what it was.

"You know," Chevreuse continued. "If those festive terrorists have any sense of occasion at all, they'll target the Repast."

"I had considered that," Athos agreed.

Her face broke into a grin. Finally, there was some colour back in her cheeks. "Want to be my date? I'm going to need help getting around."

"I'm not carrying you," he said firmly.

But that wasn't a no.

SOUP COURSE: ARAMIS IS DROWNING & PRINCE ALEK BITES OFF MORE THAN HE CAN CHEW.

Aramis had done many strange things in service to Crown and Solar System, but flicking through a hastily printed copy of the Tourist Guide to Valorous Festivals and Holidays was new to her.

It had illustrations. And she was the last person to be cynical about other people's religious beliefs, but it all seemed so stupid.

Half of the references to Winterlight were poetry, which was all very well – Aramis was fond of poetry under most circumstances – but not overly informative.

"And the rains fall, to renew and refresh, to wash away our tears," mused Porthos, consulting her own copy of the slim booklet. Treville had printed multiple copies and passed them out to all her Musketeers on duty today, for reference and research. "What does that even mean?"

"It rains a lot on Valour," Aramis said, turning another page of epigraphs that were not nearly informative enough in predicting what new fun act of sabotage was going to be perpetrated upon Paris Satellite today.

"What, it always rains on the third day of Joyeux? I mean, Winterlight, whatever. Every single time?"

"To hear Athos talk about it, it rains on Valour every day," Aramis muttered.

"Athos never talks about his home planet."

"He has twice, in five years. And both times, he complained about it raining."

Porthos considered this. "Do we need to entertain the

possibility that this festive terrorism is specifically happening to annoy Athos?"

"Oh, that's what I need," Aramis huffed. "Two paranoid best friends. Wonderful." If it was happening specifically to annoy anyone, it probably would be Athos. He had that sort of luck.

They stood at ease, beside their two musket-class darts, in the section of the Lunar Palais Primary Dock reserved for royal transportation. Major Claudine Jussac and two other red-jacketed pilots stood a little way from them, in front of the Church's own sabre-class darts.

The Regence Royal, the Cardinal and their party were late, which meant that the levels of irritable tension bouncing between the Sabres and the Musketeers had reached dangerous levels, despite the fact that Aramis herself had been behaving perfectly. Calm, polite, restrained.

Sadly, Porthos' continual filthy looks and Jussac's inability to let anything drop made up for her own restraint.

So Aramis bantered with Porthos as much as possible, to distract her from the cranky Sabres. Hopefully they would get through today without starting a riot.

Filling the air with pointless banter and Elemental research also allowed Aramis less time to worry about the end of her relationship with Chev, though in truth she spent a lot more time fretting about Athos. She had to hope he would find something in that hospice to keep himself occupied. Athos left alone with his own thoughts for a whole day was almost as dangerous as Athos attacked by mind-altering nano coffee forcing him to see visions of a traumatic former marriage.

"Heads up," Porthos said, as the door at the far end spiralled open, and the royal group approached.

Lalla-Louise Renard Royal was a beautiful sylph of a woman with sharp intelligence and a talented wit when she wasn't ground down with exhaustion from public appearances. On days like today, when their beloved leader was charming and bright-eyed, Aramis remembered all over again that the Regence of the Solar System was *exactly her type.*

She considered it a point of honour that she had never mentioned this fact to either Porthos or Athos. For the sake of their blood pressure, they must never know.

As they approached, the Regence teased the Cardinal in an arch tone of voice. "Three ships, your Eminence? I didn't realise you required quite such an entourage. I'm afraid her Grace the Duchess will think me terribly modest in only providing two for my own needs."

The Cardinal was caught between embarrassment and irritation. "Naturally, your Highness, my Sabres are duty-bound to provide for your needs as well as my own..."

"Oh, your Eminence," said the Regence with a smirk. "You're not suggesting I travel in one of your ships, are you? Why, the Musketeers would be completely out of a job, and Amiral Treville would give me such a stern lecture about the look of the thing. Though if you would like to travel together, I'm sure we can arrange some kind of compromise..."

Aramis tried hard not to roll her eyes at Porthos as the matter was settled – Porthos would take the comedy double act of the Regence and the Cardinal together in her *Hoyden,* while Aramis would escort Prince Alek, the Duchess of Buckingham and her aide Linton Gray in the *Morningstar*. The rest of the assorted priests, assistants and hangers-on in their party would be transported in the three Sabre-class darts.

Ridiculous though the scene was, it was worth it to see the quiet outrage flitting across Major Claudine Jussac's face as she realised that she and her fellow Sabres were being snubbed in the name of royal diplomacy. Even the Cardinal knew that Porthos' ship was the prettiest and most comfortable to travel in.

And oh, that meant that Aramis got to pilot the Awkward Sexual Tension Brigade that consisted of the Prince Consort and Buck the Hot Duchess My Recently Ex-Girlfriend Has Been Spending All Her Time With.

So fun all around, really.

MAIN COURSE: IF PORTHOS GETS TOO HOT, KEEP HER OUT OF THE KITCHEN.

There were many, many reasons why Porthos was in no danger of fucking Athos no matter what Aramis said or thought or did (or bet). At this stage, Porthos was pretty sure the only way it could happen was a workplace accident involving sex pollen.

Athos rarely hooked up with anyone – and when he did, he made the most self-destructive possible choices. He had a higher ratio of affair-leading-to-duel situations than anyone else in the Musketeers (Aramis once worked it out with four spreadsheets and a pie chart), and that was up against stiff competition.

It was hard to imagine that Porthos and Athos knocking boots would result in anything more dramatic than some mild embarrassment and a cordial handshake, and that basically took Porthos out of the running.

Athos couldn't be further from her type either. Porthos' love life was calm and structured. She was drawn to capable, practical men who weren't bothered by concepts like monogamy or commitment, didn't take up too much of her limited leisure time, and made themselves useful whenever she had a problem to solve.

Aramis started a spreadsheet for this, too, which was how Porthos had recently discovered that she had eight current boyfriends 'casual but active' and at least fourteen who counted as 'ex on good terms.'

Relationship drama had never appealed to her. Who could be bothered? Porthos got into enough duels over political differences, the Sabre vs. Musketeer divide and, well, Athos, without adding her love-life into the mix.

She'd like to be able to say that her perfect, bulletproof casual boyfriend system was the reason that she and Athos were safe from each other, forever and ever. But the truth was more complicated than that.

She had already met the man that she was going to screw up her perfect bulletproof system for, and it was driving her up the wall with frustration.

An unexpected encounter with Chef Coquenard while he was pinching festive greenery for his table decorations was bad enough, but a known-in-advance meeting with him in his kitchen, which he ruled with a firm voice and a devastatingly artistic pair of hands, was lethal.

"And here, the poached duck with basil," he said. Porthos opened her mouth obediently and was rewarded by a warm, savoury taste filling her mouth.

She stood in the midst of the bustling marble-tiled

kitchen of the Hotel Coquenard. Technically her job was to check on the final security arrangements for the Royal Repast that was to be hosted in the main dining room in a few hours.

The Regence, Cardinal Richelieu, the Duchess of Buckingham, the Prince Consort and the rest of their party were currently at church services, with a bodyguard detail including Aramis and Jussac. Porthos had arrived here at the hotel an hour ago to discover that they were still making last minute repairs in the main foyer after damage from the previous day.

"It was in the coffee," was all that Madame Coquenard, the long-suffering but efficient hotel owner-manager told her, before sweeping off to hurry up the workmen and ensure everything was perfect when the Regence and her people arrived.

Porthos had checked with the hotel security, examined the automated systems to her satisfaction, and now stood in a corner of the hotel's beautiful marble-tiled kitchen, being seduced with tiny mouthfuls of the feast that was to come.

The duck was definitely a seduction. She could tell by the little smile playing on the mouth of Chef Coquenard as he drew his fingers back far too slowly from her mouth. It was a seduction four years in the making, and she had an awful feeling that they were approaching the main course.

Hotel Coquenard hosted several royal events a year, thanks to their excellent service record and photogenic banquet room. Somehow it always came down to Porthos in this kitchen with this pleasant-faced chef and his extraordinary hands.

She could fall in love with hands like those. Coquenard

was a creator, an artist in the kitchen, but he didn't hesitate to do basic tasks for himself either. He would take a vegetable knife off one of his apprentices and chop it into perfect, even slices, demonstrating the technique as if he never had to think about it. Porthos had once seen him take over the job of scrubbing pots, because a dishwasher scalded her wrist and the pots had to be cleaned immediately.

Of all the things in the world, Porthos was a sucker for a man with practical skills. The fact that he liked to watch her face while she tasted whatever beautiful new food combination he had designed, did not help her to resist his charms at all.

It wasn't even the fact that he had a wife she rather liked which had held her back for – damn it, years now. It was pretty clear to everyone who knew them that Madame and Chef Coquenard had one of those marriages which had transitioned into a friendly business arrangement a long time ago.

No, the trouble was that Porthos suspected this was a man who would not fit into her usual comfortable, easy-going system. Once she had him, she wasn't going to want to let him go.

"And now, dessert?" suggested Chef Coquenard, his eyes mischievous as if he was offering more than a taste of chocolate steam upon a cube of frozen cherry juice.

Porthos opened her mouth to reply, when the kitchen door banged open. It was Athos, wearing one of his 'I am not officially a Musketeer today even if this garment is almost identical to what I wear on duty' jackets. He held the door open for Chevreuse, who came in on platinum crutches, her ankle wrapped in a medi-cast.

"Not interrupting anything, are we?" asked Chev with a cheeky gleam in her eye.

Porthos felt the urge to hurl a blancmange at her.

Chef Coquenard was delighted. Unlike every other chef Porthos had ever known, he adored being visited in his place of work. "Minister Chevreuse, I thought we were to be denied your palate today!"

"I wouldn't miss one of your meals, Remy," she said warmly, and the two of them fell into a discussion about the wine that was to be served at the Repast, and whether he was willing to discuss the various courses live on cam-feed for the viewers at home.

Porthos sidled over to Athos. "Resting up, are we?" she asked, a little sharper than she intended.

He raised both his eyebrows at her. "Still not admitting you have a crush on the chef, are we?"

She was not going to fight, if only because it would be bad timing to throw his own terrible taste in lovers in his face. She was still upset by that horrible business yesterday, and the dead husband she wished she didn't know about. "Athos – you should have stayed at the hospice."

His blue eyes went very cold. "Stop staring at me like I'm wounded, Porthos. I like to keep busy."

She accepted the point. A bored Athos was a terrible thing to inflict upon Paris Satellite. "Fair call."

"Also, I want to catch the bastards who are doing this," he added, with an edge to his voice. "Festive terrorism my arse. It stopped being a joke yesterday, and I don't fancy seeing what kind of chaos it will cause when the rains fall."

"Rain on a space station doesn't sound like a good idea," Porthos agreed. "What do we do?"

Athos tapped her on the nose. "Watch, listen, and try not to get distracted by tall men with saucy wooden spoons."

Porthos scowled.

"Move it, Athos," ordered Chevreuse all of a sudden, hurling herself at him with her crutches over one shoulder. To Porthos' surprise, Athos reached out and caught Chevreuse before she could hit the ground. How many times today had he been forced to practice that move? Chevreuse barely seemed to have noticed the near miss. "There's no water-based sprinkler system in here," she said frantically. "The hotel uses sonic wave for flame prevention. If the rains are coming down, *it's not here.*"

Well, yes. Porthos had already established this fact with Madame Coquenard, but unlike Chevreuse she hadn't seen it as a down side. Plans which required the royal family to be bait should never be anyone's first choice.

"No one uses anything but sonic wave anymore," Athos said irritably. "Unless you count…" and he stopped.

"Cathedrals," said Porthos with a sinking feeling in her stomach. "The Church of All made an edict against the use of sonic wave in places of worship, years ago. They all use vintage sprinkler systems."

Athos and Chevreuse exchanged horrified looks, and they reached for their comms in the same instant.

DESSERT COCKTAIL: TAKE THREE MUSKETEERS, DRENCH IN CHAMPAGNE & ADD TOO MUCH SPICE. SHAKE VIGOROUSLY. RESULTS MAY VARY.

It could have been worse, Athos mused. The Cardinal was furious that the ceiling of the finest cathedral in Paris had opened up and poured water down on the royal party during the ceremony of the candles. The Regence, however, took it in good humour. Prince Alek and Ambassador Buck both thought the whole matter was hilarious, especially once everyone had been dried off by sonic wave, and the two of them told the story to the assembled guests at the feast with great pantomime humour, as if they had been friends forever.

"Naturally neither of *you* got rained on," sulked Aramis, sitting between Athos and Porthos at a side table. Her hair was frizzing out of its tight "on duty" top knot.

"Just as well, since I am off duty and not even supposed to be here," said Athos calmly, sipping from a glass of champagne that cost more than his weekly rent. He glanced over at the main table. Chevreuse had clapped and smiled (with everything but her eyes) during the third retelling of the 'And then the rains came down' story. After that, she shuffled everyone around so that Buck and Prince Alek were at opposite ends of the royal table. Athos wondered if anyone else had noticed.

"It's over for today at least," said Aramis. "Though Treville has ordered the Fleet to search every church and cathedral offering night services in honour of the Repast, in case there are more planned."

"Eh, once you've saturated the most powerful people

in Paris, anything else would be an anti-climax," said Porthos.

"And no one tried to jump off a balcony, so let's call that a win," said Athos, only to receive two very dirty looks from his friends. "Too soon?"

There were six separate courses for dessert, each no larger than a medium-sized tablespoon. By the end of it, the air was alight with the scents of vanilla, rose and caramel, none of which did anything to improve the excellent champagne. Athos made sure that the champagne felt duly appreciated while everyone else flirted with tiny tortes and sorbet spheres.

As dessert gave way to after-dinner dancing, Athos stayed at the bar. Aramis found several dance partners despite being officially on duty, and Porthos was simultaneously attempting to catch and avoid the attention of Chef Coquenard, a warning sign of something Athos did not want to think closely about.

He found his eyes flitting far too often to the unassuming Mr Linton Gray, who did not dance except when it looked as if Prince Alek was about to approach the Duchess of Buckingham, at which point he offered his hand rather quickly to his boss and whirled her around the dance floor.

"So I'm not the only one with a crush," Porthos said lightly, passing him.

Athos frowned. "I don't have a *crush*. I'm trying to figure him out."

"That's what they all say." Porthos picked up his champagne glass and drank a mouthful.

"There's something about him that doesn't fit."

Porthos smiled at him over the rim of his own glass. "Ask him to dance and maybe you'll find out." She pulled a coin out of somewhere and tossed it idly back and forth. "Heads or tails. Heads, you dance with Mr Gray."

"Tails, you tell Chef Coquenard you fancy the apron off him," Athos replied sharply.

Porthos scowled, and gave him his drink back. "No bet."

"That's my girl."

Five minutes later, Porthos was dancing with the chef, and gave Athos a challenging look as they swept past him. He ignored it.

"Hey," said Chevreuse, joining him at the bar.

"I am not going to carry you around the dance floor," Athos said firmly.

"Wasn't going to ask. I've done my duty, wined and dined the Ambassador and made sure that all the necessary media snaps have been taken. Not that anyone's going to be looking at cam feeds of polite smiles on the steps of the hotel when there's footage doing the rounds of the Regence and the Cardinal being rained on in church." Something like pain crossed her face. "There's a pic of Prince Alek in a wet shirt that's going to go viral."

"Congratulations?" Athos ventured. He wasn't entirely sure what the point was of this particular interaction.

Chevreuse gave him a tired look. "You get to keep me company while I drown my sorrows about the sports-related disaster that I've avoided thinking about all day."

"That's within my skillset," Athos agreed. "Champagne or some sort of vaguely festive rum punch?"

Chevreuse leaned across the bar, making eye contact with the bartender. "I would like a mojito the size of my head, thank you very much."

Athos continued to pay his respects to the champagne. "You're off the clock? Completely disinterested in anything to do with royal PR?"

"Completely," Chevreuse said with deep conviction.

"So the fact that the Prince Consort is currently eye-fucking the Duchess of Buckingham across the dance floor doesn't bother you at all?"

Chevreuse swore and looked discreetly over one shoulder. Athos didn't have to follow her gaze to know that Prince Alek and Buck were dancing closely with their respective partners, but making steamy eye contact with each other at the same time. They'd been doing it for the last three dances. "I hate everything," said Chevreuse, banging her head lightly on Athos' shoulder. The large, icy mojito arrived in front of her, and she stared balefully at it. "I should have ordered one big enough to climb inside. Do you think anyone's noticed them?"

Athos should not be finding this amusing. "*I* noticed, and I am the person in the room who cares least about royal gossip."

"You make a good point." Chevreuse took a deep swallow from her drink and then pushed it away so she could lay her forehead against the bar. "This job is going to kill me. Time to run away and join the circus."

Athos nodded in sympathy, and they drank together in silence for a while.

By the time Chevreuse was halfway down her mojito,

Prince Alek and Buck had managed to dance together once more, almost setting the nearest hover-chandelier on fire with the vibes between them before they were tactfully separated by other dance partners. They continued to meet each other's gaze at any opportunity.

"I thought her being here would be great," Chevreuse moaned, darting occasional looks over her shoulder. "We were friends, years ago. I thought, Buck's a good sort, it will be fun to have her around. Maybe she can even take over some of my duties while I'm resting up from this bloody leg injury, since Ambassadors can…" She stopped talking all of a sudden, and grabbed for the clamshell in her silver handbag. She called up a series of legislative papers, and read through them in silence.

It was the most peaceful moment Athos had enjoyed all day. He motioned for a refill of his glass, and idly watched Porthos refusing to dance again with Chef Coquenard, who was incapable of taking her stubbornness as any kind of insult. The chef smiled, bowed and kissed her hand.

Someone was playing a long game, and Athos couldn't tell which of them it was.

"I am the queen of everything," Chevreuse hooted, smacking her clamshell closed. She chugged the last of her mojito. "I am the goddess of loopholes, and they should build a fucking statue in my honour."

"It's your modesty I most respect," Athos said gravely.

"I can't play in tomorrow's final, and we can't use a sub without us losing the 'unbeatable' record, right?" Chevreuse said, about to burst out of her skin.

"Possibly I'm not the ideal audience to which you should be making this revelation. I didn't even care that much about fleur-de-lis *before* I started drinking tonight."

"Good point." She turned away from him, placing a call through her clamshell. "Su!" she shrieked into it as her fleur-de-lis teammate who wasn't the Prince Consort came up on the screen. "You're never going to guess how brilliant I am. We can have it all! We use Buck as the substitute. Ambassadorial privilege means she can replace any member of the government in a public appearance as if she was that person. It's a goddammed loophole and we are going to sail all the way through it to victory, baby!"

Conrad Su was equally excited, based on the loud exclamations and swearing that came out of the screen. The two of them made plans for the following day. Chev closed her clamshell in triumph and ordered a second mojito to celebrate.

"I don't mean to put a dampener on this," said Athos. "But do you think it's a good idea that our esteemed Ambassador spends any more time with his Royal Highness? Where a best case scenario means they will bond further by sharing the passionate afterglow of victory?"

Chevreuse blinked several times, and then groaned. "I hate everything again."

Athos sipped his champagne. "Tough choice."

"No, no it's not," she said after a long moment. "Damn it. I work twenty hours a day for these bloody royals. Fleur-de-lis is the one thing I have that's *mine* and even then I spend half of it worrying about press conferences and cam feeds so the Prince comes out looking like a fucking hero. They owe me this. They owe me this one game, and I'm going to take it."

"The pain meds are wearing off, aren't they?"

"Shut up. Yes."

"Drink faster. It helps."

CHAPTER 4
MISRULE
(THE DANCE OF THE ELEMENTS)

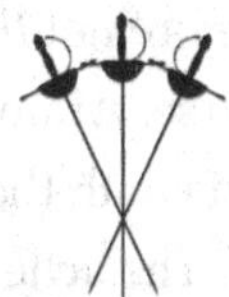

ATHOS hates to watch cinquefoil, brutal mishmash that it is, but he will admit to an appreciation for fleur-de-lis. There's a calm precision to the game, to the spinning of the poles and the intensity of player against player. It's almost as good as fencing, but no one would be crazy enough to fence in zero gravity.

He has often thought that he would love to get a foil into Chevreuse's hands, but she is too dedicated to her own sport to be tempted by something as tame as swordwork.

This a strange match to watch. The Emerald Knights are still the Emerald Knights without Chev, but Buck is so different, all passion and thrust where Chevreuse is restraint and brutal precision.

Buck would make a terrible fencer, but she is astounding in the air.

ARAMIS is not surprised when Chevreuse insists on watching the game with them. They don't have a ticket for her, but she squeezes between Porthos and Athos, her legs slung across their laps. Aramis can feel Chev's feet brushing against her hip, and she wants to kiss her.

Aramis misses Chevreuse like breathing. She's still here, so close, and yet they're not *that* anymore. Are they anything? Friends, of course, Aramis has always been good about staying friends with the women she loves.

It's different this time. The ache is different, perhaps because she started missing Chev even before they broke up. They were terrible together, at least half of the time. But when it was good, it was so fucking good, and now Aramis does not know where to go next.

(Maybe it's time, maybe this is a sign that the Musketeers aren't for her any more, she always wanted to be a priest… this has been a distraction along the way.)

She could never have kissed her here in the stadium like she wants to right now. They would never have risked that kind of public affection.

Aramis knows it must be killing Chev to be in the audience and not in the tank. They're friends now, which means Aramis can reach out and squeeze her hand to comfort her, if she wants to. It's too soon, though. She can't quite trust herself to do it right.

Friends is fine. Aramis can do this. Eventually the ache will go away.

PORTHOS loves the manic grunt of cinquefoil, the mess

and the sweat of five-on-five TeamJoust, with its blood and bruises. That's a real sport.

It would probably be a bad idea to let the Prince Consort play a version of the game that would smash his pretty face on a regular basis. Chevreuse is living proof that even the prissy fleur-de-lis version of TeamJoust does not guarantee the safety of its players.

Chevreuse is heavier than she looks, sprawled across Porthos' lap, with her head tipped back against Athos' shoulder. She's trying too hard, cheering every match point and making silly faces at the cam, letting everyone know what a good sport she is about not playing today. It's not fooling anyone.

Is it too soon for Porthos to admit that she never really liked Chev? She never thought she was good for Aramis. They were in love, anyone could see that, but they didn't make each other happy. The fights had been getting worse, the screaming and throwing things, and now they have this – pretending they can still be friends torture. It's no fun for anyone.

Aramis says something that Porthos can't hear and she turns her head just in time to catch a sly "Four days to go," in the curve of her ear.

"Four days to what?"

"Till the end of Joyeux."

Porthos turns and stares at her friend, who pretends to have her attention on the game. "The what now? Is this still about your stupid bet?" Surely it's only friends in happy relationships who devise fiendish schemes to matchmake their other friends, not those in the midst of messy break ups?

Aramis looks gleeful. "It wouldn't kill you to sleep with him."

Chevreuse catches part of that, because of course she does. "Sleep with who?"

"Me, probably," says Athos, who misses nothing. "I'm a catch."

"I hate you all," says Porthos, her face going hot all over. "And also, never going to happen." She raises her fist towards Athos and he bumps knuckles with her in solidarity.

Platonic fistbumps for the win.

ARAMIS watches the Emerald Knights win. They win the game, and take out the record as the first fleur-de-lis team in history to have an unbeaten season.

It breaks Aramis into pieces to watch Chevreuse screaming with delight and pride. They actually could have got away with kissing in public today, and no one would have thought it was anything romantic. Chev smooches Porthos and tugs on Athos' beard, and when Prince Alek runs over to pick her up and take her to the podium with him, she beats him on the back of the shoulder blades and rubs her bright green makeup all over his face.

Chevreuse and Aramis could totally have got away with kissing in public in this moment, but that's not going to happen because they broke up two days ago and there's a heavy feeling in the pit of Aramis' stomach that won't go away.

It was a good game, and she and Chev spent the whole

of it practicing their 'just friends now' skills but seeing her girlfriend (ex-girlfriend) up there with her teammates and that bloody trophy feels like the end of something.

Maybe the end happened a long time ago, and Aramis was too damned stupid to see it.

(This would never have happened if she was a priest, she would have her life together and stop hurling ridiculous, doomed relationships at it)

She leans into Porthos, who is still clapping and cheering, and says "Next season, can we go to the cinquefoil games instead?"

Porthos hooks one arm around Aramis' neck in a hug that's mostly comforting. "You'll get over it," she says.

"Don't want to," Aramis sulks.

ATHOS hates Misrule. Joyeux is his least favourite of everything. What the hell is the point of celebrating midwinter traditions on a space station? But he hates Misrule the most.

This was true even before the whole festive terrorism thing turned Joyeux from an annual annoyance to something that was actively trying to kill him.

(Winterlight was just as bad at this time of year, and what does 'the dance of the elements' even mean? Planetside it was an excuse for foolish behaviour just like Misrule here in space. As if the concept of Misrule was ever going to be a good idea for people who live in artificial oxygen and gravity)

Athos volunteered to be on duty for the ball weeks ago, because he thought it would be less annoying than being forced to have fun by his so-called friends who have never respected his distaste for holidays.

But no, this is the actual worst. If he wasn't on duty, he could slip away home and/or get drunk, but instead he is patrolling the ornamental gardens outside the Palace, which means tripping over copulating couples in nearly every rosebush.

He is not getting paid enough to deal with the blatantly underage girls with their glittery boobs hanging out of space dragon costumes. Two of them vomit into a virtual fishpond while another holds back their hair and sings show tunes in an off key voice.

It is 22:00 hours. Everyone in the solar system is less sober than Athos. The festive terrorists have yet to make their mark on the fourth day of Joyeux.

He almost hopes their plan is to blow up the Palace.

"Athos," says a quiet voice in his private comm line, the one that usually only Aramis and Porthos use. He frowns for a moment before realising that it is Chevreuse. "Are you still on duty?"

"Will I regret saying yes?"

"Don't be a smart-arse. Are you here?"

"Near the north balcony." He heads up the winding steps to the balcony, and stands at the rail until Chevreuse eases her way out of the double doors to join him. "Assassination attempts?" she asks in a brittle voice.

"Zero so far."

"My favourite number." Chevreuse is more tired than Athos has ever seen her. Worn thin, wrung out, and pissed off. She leans heavily on the single stick that she has been using today instead of the crutches. The medipatches have mostly put her leg back together again by now, but she'll have the limp for a day or two. "I need to beg a favour, but you can't ask why, or request any details, and afterwards we never talk about it again."

Athos' eyebrows almost disappear off the top of his face.

"Also, don't make that expression."

"I can't help my face."

"Athos, *please*."

"Tell me," he says gravely. It's not like tonight can get any worse.

Chevreuse passes him a small slip of paper with a series of time codes written out for him. "I need you to perform some digital surgery on one of the internal security cam feeds. Preferably without looking at what's on it."

Athos stares at the paper – actual paper, ensuring no electronic trace – and then back at her. He's talking to Minister Chevreuse now, not Chev the hellcat pole defence who crashed into their lives because of her passion for Aramis. "Tell me I'm not committing treason," he sighs.

He knows what this is – the shape of it, at least. Anyone who saw the way Prince Alek and Buck were staring at each other yesterday might suspect why some cam footage now has to be deleted.

"I'm pretty sure it doesn't qualify as treason," Chevreuse says after a moment's hesitation.

"That's not as reassuring as you think it is."

"I'm going to tell the Regence the whole story," she promises him. "But believe me, it will go down better without anyone having the chance to review the visuals."

That doesn't sound likely, but it's her funeral. "Fine," Athos agrees. "I'll do it. Of course I will." He sticks the paper in his pocket.

Chevreuse looks as if she had expected him to put up more of an argument. "Just like that?"

"I trust you," he drawls, putting as much sarcasm into it as he can.

For a moment, he thinks she is going to hug him, and he steps back out of range hastily. But Chevreuse gives him a look instead, a small smile, like she knows exactly what is going on in his head.

He doesn't trust her that much.

PORTHOS blames Misrule. That is the only explanation for the man melting chocolate in Porthos' kitchen.

Bonnie is away visiting her family for the holiday, and Porthos is celebrating, apparently, by letting the man she promised herself she would never sleep with take serious liberties with Bonnie's stove top.

Can she blame Bonnie for this? If her engie was still here, Porthos would not have invited Chef Coquenard up for a drink when she bumped into him in the Misrule crowd that has transformed Marie Antoinette Esplanade into a dancing, grinding flashmob of poor decisions.

She might at least have tossed a coin, left it up to chance instead of plunging forward with something she's not sure she wants to finish.

They've had an in-depth conversation about life and the universe. She's still dizzy with the revelation that he and Madame Coquenard are divorced, have been for years, that Porthos' interpretation of their relationship as one of a friendly business arrangement is literally true.

This is the worst thing that could have happened.

Because Coquenard is here, right here in her kitchen, telling her about the historical origins of hot chocolate as he adds chilli and paprika to the smooth liquid in the pan, and then takes it off the heat to add cream and milk.

Has she mentioned his shoulders? She certainly hasn't stopped thinking about them in the last half hour or so. He fills the room, not just with his large frame but with his soft, deep voice, and there is no reason at all why she shouldn't drag him into her bed right now.

Except that he's still talking, and she can't stop smiling, and oh, this is bad. This is catastrophic. Joyeux should be banned.

They drink brandy in large tumblers while they wait for the chocolate, and Porthos has lost track of how many times they have refilled each other's glasses.

She first met Remy Coquenard four years ago, and she promised herself that she would always keep him at arm's length. That plan has worked so very well for all this time and now she can't even remember why it was so important.

He serves her hot chocolate in her own tiny mugs, the ones that Aramis complains about because they're too small for anything but the sharp, strong coffee that only Athos likes to drink. Tonight, the cups are perfect for rich, spiced chocolate, and Porthos sips hers until her tongue is soothed and spiky all at once from the combination of flavours.

"Pollina," he says softly. No one else calls her that, not any more. Pol, on occasion, she quite likes that Pol stays with her even now, but never Pollina. She should hate it, but it sounds so good in his voice. Everything sounds good in his voice. "Ask me to stay, and I'll make you breakfast."

"I hate breakfast," she lies, but kisses him anyway.

She fists her hands against his neck, and he backs her against the wall. The taste of hot chocolate heats up in both of their mouths. *Joyeux*, Porthos decides in a fierce thought before all rational thought melts away completely. *Joyeux will always taste like this.*

ATHOS finds Chevreuse in the gardens, alone. She sits on a bench, her walking stick stretched across her knees and her head tipped back as if she's actually listening to the music that filters out of the plexi-glass doors of the Palace. Her hair is still emerald green. Was the game really today? It seems a long time ago.

"Done," Athos says, and drops on to the bench next to her.

"Thank you," sighs Chevreuse.

He bumps his shoulder companionably against hers. "I suppose you know what you're doing."

"Fuck, I hope so."

They sit in silence for a long moment.

"It was a good game today," Athos says. "Your plan to use the Duchess of Buckingham was inspired."

"If I never see that woman again it will be too bloody soon," Chevreuse grates out.

Her venom is surprising, but only to a point. "I thought she was a friend of yours," says Athos.

"Did you watch the footage before you deleted it?"

"I think it's in all our best interests if I don't answer that question."

"Good call," says Chevreuse. She is drowning in some private misery, and Athos would rather be anywhere than here.

"Look," he says, turning to her, and she turns to him in the same moment and oh, bloody hell. This is not a possibility he has ever contemplated. She is off limits, for so many reasons.

Chevreuse leans into him, and their mouths brush together for a moment. It's not a kiss, but it could be. It's a long time since Athos has felt such a genuine tug of *want* towards another human being, but right now he wants her like breathing, like wine.

Of all the things he has ever done to push his friends away, this is a line he has never crossed. He's an addict, not a fool.

Athos lets his kiss slide on to her cheek instead, and then pulls away altogether. Chevreuse gives him a knowing, shaky smile.

"Look at you," she breathes. "Making good decisions. I'm almost proud."

"Well, it is Misrule," Athos reminds her. "The world is supposed to be upside down." He considers offering her the platonic fistbump that he and Porthos share, but decides she is unlikely to find it funny any time soon.

ARAMIS is off duty and loving it. The pulse of the music, the freedom to dance and flirt and not hang around waiting for a few stolen moments with her (former) girlfriend.

Aramis is not at the Palace tonight. Musketeers have a standing invitation for the Misrule Ball, as do all members of the Royal Fleet. But she doesn't fancy rubbing shoulders with the Cardinal's Sabres all night, or getting her dance on in the same building where Chevreuse is working her usual PR magic.

So Aramis is in Marie Antoinette Esplanade in the heart of Paris Satellite. It started out as a street party with attitude, and somewhere around the third DJ of the night transformed into a deeper, dirtier celebration of Misrule than the Palace could possibly offer.

This is Paris on a plate. Beautiful and professional by day, a sweat-drenched party animal at night.

Aramis grinds against a unicorn, surrounded by a dazzling group of young women wearing fake Mendaki tentacles and hot pants. It's loud and hot and fast. The unicorn has a gorgeous mask, all satin and beads and a long, curling horn jutting out from her forehead. Only her mouth stands out beneath the mask, slick and wet.

Aramis dances like it's her last night alive.

Her breath puffs out like steam as the temperature drops in the bar, far too rapidly to be natural. Aramis' eyes are closed when she feels the first snowflakes on her face.

ATHOS thinks it might be a minute, perhaps two minutes, since he and Chevreuse did not kiss each other on the mouth. Somewhere, a clock strikes midnight. They are far too close to each other, and still not kissing. It's a frozen moment of tension, broken only by the echoes of the deep clock chimes.

"SNOW, ATHOS!" screams a voice over his comm. It's too loud, enough that his first impulse is to rip the stud out of his wrist, but it's worse than that, because it's Aramis.

"What?" he says, lifting the wrist in the time-honoured gesture for 'taking a call.' Chevreuse politely glances away.

"I'm in Marie Antoinette and it's motherfucking snowing all over the plaza, like actual snow, and it's settling, I think it's for real!" Aramis howls. She sounds off her face, but that doesn't stop the guilty feeling that maybe somehow she knows what nearly happened here.

Chev blows Athos a kiss and heads her way back to the party on her walking stick, her head held high. She doesn't look back. They're racking up the good decisions between them, tonight. They deserve some sort of prize.

"It's midnight," says Athos, breathing out and letting his shoulders slump back against the bench. "It's tomorrow."

"SNOW STARTED LIKE TEN MINUTES AGO," Aramis shouts, and he can hear the buzz of the crowd behind her. She's not shouting at him because she knows he nearly snogged her girlfriend (ex-girlfriend), she is just trying to be heard. "It's yesterday's thing, but maybe it's today's thing too, because it's snowing all over and it's not stopping and can we totally build a snowman?"

Athos wants to laugh, because it's that or punch himself in the face. "I'm on Lunar Palais, I'm too far away to build a snowman with you. Call Porthos."

"Can't, Porthos is GETTING LAID," Aramis hoots.

"There's chocolate involved, it's a whole kinky chef thing. Don't call her, she's busy."

"What would I do without you to keep me up to date on these developments?"

"It's a new day, Athos. Happy fucking Joyeux!"

"Happy Joyeux to you too," he says, and almost means it.

"I love you, honeypie!"

"You're ridiculous," he says, but he can't stop his mouth twitching into a smile.

Aramis and Porthos saved him, they keep saving him. Their friendship is the closest he will ever come to loving anyone after the broken pieces of his former life, after Auden, after the world he left behind. Athos would rather cut off an arm than hurt either of them.

"It's Amends!" Aramis howls into the comm. "It's tomorrow, that's Amends!"

How fiendishly appropriate. A day for making reparations for past sins, and renewing the bonds of friendship. Can Athos claim not sleeping with Chevreuse as his holiday activity for that day too? "Not on Valour," he tells Aramis. "On Valour it's the fifth day of Winterlight."

"Valour is stupid!" Aramis howls through the comm. "Your planet is stupid, Athos."

"Not arguing that point."

"Five days of winter is too many winter!"

"Winter lasts longer than five days," he reminds her.

"What happens on the today of Winterlight?"

Athos breathes out. He remembers real snow. The chill of it, the frost-tipped trees, the fog of his warm breath on a bright, cloudless day. He could have lived without ever seeing snow again, and now he's going to have to walk through the damn stuff to get to his quarters, if he goes home to Paris after his shift ends. Since the alternative is staying here to make extremely bad decisions with a woman he needs to never be alone with again, he is definitely going home to Paris.

"Breathing the air," he says into the comm. "Day five of Winterlight is breathing the air."

Aramis laughs hysterically at him for half a minute. "Only on Valour would they have a whole holiday devoted to breathing."

"Only on Valour," he agrees.

"Valour is stupid, Athos."

"Good night, sweetness."

On his way back through the party, after signing out for the end of his shift, Athos spots Mr Linton Gray standing near the bar, observing the festivities through calm, uninvolved eyes. His boss, the Duchess of Buckingham, is nowhere in sight.

Athos finds himself slowing down, offering a nod to the other man whom he suspects has had almost as difficult a night as he has. "Do you ever wish a day could be entirely struck from the records?" he asks gravely.

Mr Gray flinches as if he had not expected to be addressed, and then a slow smile passes over his face, making him look altogether more interesting than when he is playing the invisible man. "All the time," he replies.

"Misrule has always seemed like an exceptionally bad idea," Athos says, which is perhaps an obvious statement, but prolongs the conversation.

Since when did that seem like such an appealing notion? He can't seem to move away as he originally intended.

"Isn't that rather the point?" asks Mr Gray.

It's a challenge, but it makes Athos smile. Is this flirting? Compared to the horrendous possibility of seducing Chevreuse and living with those consequences, the appeal is obvious. Linton Gray offers no drama whatsoever.

The sensible, practical decision would be to flirt with no one, to talk with no one, and to go home.

"Would you like to have a drink with me?" Gray asks.

Athos considers the possibility, and lets it go. "Another time."

But he smiles, to show that he means it and after a moment, Linton Gray smiles back at him.

CHAPTER 5
AMENDS
(BREATHING THE AIR)

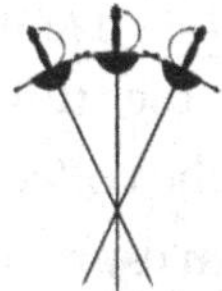

t was 08:00 hours on the morning of Amends, and two of the three Musketeers known to their colleagues as 'the inseparables' were severely hungover.

The other one was Athos.

"Your face is alarming," groaned Porthos, struggling to lift her face from the table at the canteen outside Treville's office. They usually avoided this place, because all three of them had a tendency to pick fights when they socialised too often with Musketeers besides each other. They were only here because the Stellar Concourse, Marie Antoinette Esplanade and a bunch of their other favourite places on Paris Satellite were currently under several feet of snow.

"It's the smile that makes it creepy," said Aramis, wincing as Athos placed a cup of tea in a china cup and saucer before Porthos, a double shot chai latte in front of Aramis, and then a plate of savoury pastries between them to share. "Food. Athos, you don't approve of food in the morning."

"Don't worry about me," said Athos, breaking pieces

off a croissant and actually putting them in his mouth. "I wasn't drinking last night."

His two friends stared at him in mutual horror. "Misrule was yesterday," Aramis said finally. "The solar system isn't still supposed to be topsy turvy." She shook her hair, which she hadn't managed to capture into its usual severe topknot. Glitter fell out of it. "Damn it, I had two showers this morning, where does the stuff keep coming from?"

"I see you're back on the coffee," grouched Porthos.

Athos knocked back an espresso with every appearance of cheer. "Life's too short to be without," he said in a saintly voice. " I drank vegetable juice when I first woke up. Genuine vitamins."

Aramis rested her forehead gingerly on the table. "I woke up with a unicorn between my thighs."

Porthos patted her friend on one shoulder. "Never tell me more details. Never ever." She herself had awoken with Chef Coquenard pressed against her back, and it had been all she could do to convince him that no, she did not want him to feed her hangover, no matter how many sweet promises he made about blueberry pancakes.

"You three, in here, NOW!" roared Amiral Treville from her doorway. No one else in the canteen even turned a hair because 'you three' always meant one specific group of Musketeers.

Porthos trailed after Athos and Aramis into Treville's plexi-glass office.

"Scrape yourselves off the floor, ratbags, I need you for a – what the HELL happened to Athos?"

Athos smiled sweetly at her. "Made good choices during Misrule, boss. Also, I had a healthy breakfast. I might make a habit of it."

"He's doing it to spite us, boss," sighed Aramis. "We're trying not to be traumatised, but we might need to put in for therapy after the festive season."

Treville folded her arms. "I hate that I trust you three enough to send you on regular missions. I have grey hairs with your names on them. Look!"

Athos pretended to look and then gave Treville a charming smile. "Only adds to your mature-aged allure, boss. It's distinguished."

A low rumble that might have been a growl emerged from the depths of Treville's barrel-shaped chest. No one was fooled. They all knew Athos was her favourite.

"We'll try to keep him from upsetting people," Porthos promised, and then thought about what she had just said. "We'll keep him away from people."

"The Red Hammers have detained a large number of suspects in the Winterlight-Joyeux terrorism case," Treville said, forging ahead with their mission despite the fact that Athos being chipper might well herald the beginning of an apocalypse.

"Hang on," said Athos. "Isn't that *our* jurisdiction? This case is about royal security, not..."

"We share responsibility for the safety of Paris Satellite with the Church of All, Captain-Lieutenant Athos," Treville said sharply. "And given that eight different places of worship found themselves knee-deep in fucking SNOW overnight, the Regence did not hesitate to give her Eminence the Cardinal free rein to do whatever she wished in pursuit of the culprits."

"That means the Musketeers and the Sabres and Hammers are all going to be tripping over themselves until this case is solved, sir!" protested Aramis.

"Yes," said Treville without hesitation. "Too bloody right, Aramis. Suck it up and make the best of it. As I was saying, her Eminence has gracefully allowed me to send representative Musketeers to observe the interrogations." She paused, and looked meaningfully at the three of them. "For the sake of peaceful co-operation between the fleets."

Porthos could not quite wrap her head around this. "And you chose us, sir? As your representatives. To keep the peace with the Red Hammers and the Sabres." She stopped short of asking, *have you met us*?

"Indeed," said Treville, looking innocent and glare-y at the same time. "Any reason why I should not choose you?"

"We do," said Aramis, and then stopped. "I mean, no one in this room has forgotten that most of the disciplinary marks on our files have to do with duelling out of hours, with the Sabres and Hammers. Right?"

Treville raised her eyebrows very high, as if this was the first she had heard of such a thing.

"Amiral Treville," said Athos, clearing his throat. Shock had pushed him through outrage and concern all the way to polite. Porthos silently added that information to her mental list of ways to manage Athos in an emergency. "Can I ask – is our mission to observe the interrogations impartially, or is our mission to severely piss off the Cardinal?"

Their commanding officer did not smile, but something tugged at the side of her mouth which might resolve itself into a smile once all three of them were at a safe distance. She reached out, and patted Athos gently on the cheek. "I am as committed to finding the truth behind these attacks as anyone. But tying the three of you up with a red ribbon for the Cardinal is the closest I'll get to giving myself a Joyeux present this year. So let's just say, I'm keeping my options open."

"I don't know whether to be insulted or impressed," Athos said, obviously still contemplating the complex wiles of Amiral Treville as they made their way over to the Armoury. "Damn, she's good."

Several public walkways were still caked with snow, though many were in the process of being cleared.

"Whoever is doing this Winterlight shit has a sense of humour," decided Porthos. "A nasty sense of humour at times, sure," she added, thinking of the horrors that Day 2 and the coffee had inflicted on them all. "But – the rest of it has been almost harmless. Frivolous."

Aramis made a humphing sound. "The snow was pretty awesome," she conceded. "But we can't afford to relax."

"Nothing we've done so far has prevented any of it," Athos pointed out, his hands buried deep in the pockets of his blue Musketeer jacket. "At least it will all be over within two days."

Porthos cheered up at that. "And Aramis will finally have to pay up from that stupid bet about us sleeping together!" She reached her hand over for the customary platonic fistbump and noticed an odd expression on Athos' face. "Did it stop being funny? Did I miss a memo?"

"Nope, all good, nothing to see here," Athos said

quickly, bumping her knuckles solemnly with his own, and walking a little faster.

Huh. Weird.

The Cardinal was nowhere in sight when Porthos, Athos and Aramis reported to the Armoury, which was probably just as well as it reduced the likelihood that one or all of them would end up on charges for sacrilege or whatever else they threw at you for getting mouthy with a religious leader.

Even Aramis had been known to get a bit sarcastic where Her Eminence was concerned, and she was the most religiously conservative of the three.

Claudine Jussac was in charge, which was exactly what they didn't need. "You three," she said with a malicious look as she came over to swipe them through security. "Was Treville hoping to turn this into a street brawl? I wasn't aware you had any other skills collectively."

"We're at your disposal, Captain," said Athos, little ray of sunshine that he was today.

Porthos was over today already.

"As observers, you are required to *not* interfere with our interrogations," Jussac said, as if she wasn't loving this. "I have just the place for you." She led them to an operations room featuring several screens, each looking into a different grim cell. "So many suspects to get through, we'll be working them simultaneously. I hope that won't be too confusing." She pushed a tablet into Porthos' hand and left them to it.

Aramis leaned over Porthos' shoulder, scanning the tablet. "That's a lot of names," she said.

Porthos scrolled down, and down, and down. "There are hundreds," she said faintly. "Hundreds of – how can these all be suspects?"

Athos reached out, and took the tablet from her, running his eye over the list. "They're not suspects," he said finally, handing it back. "At least, not for any intelligent reason. That is a list of practicing Elementals on Paris Satellite."

"How do you know?" Aramis asked, and then bit her lip when Athos shot her a cynical look. "Are you saying that the Cardinal has taken this as an excuse to harass them all?"

"Or to ask questions she normally wouldn't get to ask," said Athos, glaring at the empty cells on the screens. "And we get to observe it all. You were curious about religious differences, Aramis? Now you get a front seat to a live action theology debate."

"That's not fair," she snapped.

"Isn't it?" His mouth was a grim line, and he had lost all of that morning's humour. "Nothing about this is fair."

Stick a fork in her, Porthos was done.

Everything about her that was kind or good had dribbled out of her ears hours ago.

Ninety four suspects had been questioned today, and the Musketeers had been able to do nothing but witness the interrogations. Athos, she noticed, barely listened to the answers given by the suspects, many of whom were defensive and scared. He had, however, taken careful note of the questions being asked. Porthos followed his lead.

Aramis had watched and listened quietly, taking no notes, and occasionally fetching refreshments for them all, as some kind of unspoken apology to Athos.

By the end of the day, the emotions in the room were so fraught that Porthos wanted to set fire to everything.

She needed home and sleep and whatever good thing Bonnie was cooking. She needed uncomplicated sex with one of the various uncomplicated men in her life, which described all of them except for the Chef she was definitely not freaking out about. (Him, she wanted to wrap her arms around while she talked about her day, and that was so not happening, not today or ever.)

Hopefully, her next work shift would involve something calming and predictable like her actual job. Flying through a minefield or taking a bullet for the Regence would be preferable to this shit.

Porthos couldn't call Chef Coquenard (*not that she wanted to*). He would be prepping for evening service right about now. But there was at least half a temptation in her heart (*no, there wasn't*), to sit in a corner of his kitchen and drown herself in the scent of extravagant entrees and decadent desserts (*Porthos, you're doing denial wrong*).

She didn't wait for Athos and Aramis as she headed out of the grey walls of the Armoury, but then a text flashed through her comm, the letters coming up in a brief glowing hologram as she passed her thumb over the stud on her wrist.

ARAMIS: Hold up – ATTM

Porthos closed her eyes and groaned. What the hell

was her life, that she and Aramis got semi-regular use out of the acronym Athos Thinks Too Much?

"Rec space," she said into her comm, to Aramis and Athos both. "Ten minutes."

She strode ahead, making her way along one of the moving walkways and making for the entertainment hub at Marie Antoinette Esplanade. She paid for a rec space and started tapping in the code for their usual practice gear.

Fencing was the default recreation that Athos always chose. Aramis had the perfect body for long distance running, and liked to use that to torture the other two on the grounds that they extra-hated her other favourite choice, an unholy combination of yoga and Tai Chi.

Today was Porthos' choice, because she was here first, damn it, and she wanted to hit things.

When Aramis arrived, pushing a glassy-eyed Athos ahead of her, Porthos knew this was a good idea. She threw a pair of gloves to him, and took some satisfaction in the sharp look he gave her as he caught them.

"Make yourself useful," she challenged.

Athos nodded. "I need to —" He stopped, shaking his head. "Work through something."

"*Your brain,*" Porthos said in a weary voice. "Hit me already."

It took a solid thirty minutes of light boxing, Porthos and Aramis swapping in and out of bouts against Athos, before his face began to look more like it belonged to a person instead of a long-haul space passenger who had been deprived of sleep meds.

"Okay," he said finally, flinging the gloves to one side and pacing back and forth across the floor. "It's not any of the poor bastards we saw today. Whatever the Cardinal is up to, it's not them. This whole festive terrorism bullshit was an excuse to make things uncomfortable for Elementals. Right?"

"I hate it when he paces," said Aramis, dropping into a stretch. "It's never good when his feet think harder than the rest of him."

Porthos sprawled on the floor, gulping water from one of the bottles she had ordered. "What makes you think it's not one of the suspects?"

"Because all of this, the green and the snow and the rain – it's showboating. The only reason to pull off such ridiculous tricks on an entire space station is to get attention. Today's mass interrogation was a different kind of showboating exercise. The Cardinal didn't care about any of the people in that interrogation room, or what they had to say. She was staging it for an audience."

"Why bother?" Aramis asked.

Athos frowned and paced some more. His hand flexed back and forth like he wanted to have a sword in it, but Porthos had stored all of their pilot's slices in a locker when the other two were sparring. She stood by that decision. The last thing they needed when Athos was in a state like this was to arm him.

"Who's the audience?" Porthos chipped in.

Athos spun around, his eyes blazing. "Someone she can't touch any other way."

Porthos thought about it for a moment, and then started swearing, because of course.

"The Prince Consort," moaned Aramis. "Everyone knows that Prince Alek is from an Elemental New Aristocrat family. Her Eminence was against the marriage because of it."

"Diplomatic immunity," Porthos added. "It could be about Buck and her people."

Athos was furious, either at the universe or at himself. "We have to talk to your girlfriend, Aramis."

"Ex-girlfriend," Aramis corrected. "Can we not involve Chev in this, please? We haven't had a day apart since our break up and it's *awkward.*"

"Yes, I imagine it is," said Athos. He wasn't lost in his thoughts any more. He was terrifyingly present. "Do you know what else is awkward? She got me to destroy the fucking evidence."

"Well," said Minister Marie Chevreuse-Montbazon a few hours later, in her beautifully-furnished apartment at the Palace. Her gaze flitted from Athos to Aramis and back again, before finally landing on Porthos. "I'd ask why exactly the three of you felt this intervention was necessary, but if I'm wrong, it's going to be embarrassing."

"The Misrule footage," said Athos in a cold voice. "I need to know what was on it."

Her face closed over. "No you don't. Damn it, Athos, I should have known asking you to keep a secret meant I was automatically telling two other people."

There was an edge to Chevreuse's voice that was out of place, even considering that the three of them had ambushed her at her own apartment. Porthos looked from Athos to Chevreuse, wondering if the current situation was the only reason they had to be angry at each other.

They seemed fine at the fleur-de-lis game yesterday, as friendly as ever.

"Athos thinks you got him to cover up the Duchess of Buckingham's involvement in the festive terrorism attacks," said Aramis, sounding calm. "Please tell him he's wrong."

Chevreuse looked genuinely startled, and then she began to laugh. She almost doubled over, she was so overcome. "Oh, that would have been awesome," she said when she recovered herself. "I wish it was that." She met Athos' gaze and shook her head at him, disappointed. "Did you forget that the bastard coffee pretty much wrecked my fleur-de-lis season? I am not on the side of the mistletoe-flingers."

"I believe that you are professional enough to cover up a major diplomatic incident even if it inconveniences you," he drawled.

"Aww, Athos," said Chevreuse, batting her eyelashes. "That's actually sweet." Her face went suddenly very hard. "Fuck you, I'm not a traitor."

"So what was it, if not to do with the Winterlight attacks?" Aramis pressed.

"I'm the Minister for Royal PR, what kind of cover up would it be if I went around telling my ex and her playmates about it?" Chevreuse snapped. "This is *not* your business."

All three of them stared at her.

She stared back.

Athos broke the silence first. "Blackmail or sex scandal?"

"Neither."

"Come on, Chev."

"It had potential for either or both," she admitted reluctantly. "But it didn't get that far, thanks to some quick intervention from me and a certain Mr Linton Gray plus a completely anonymous Musketeer who was supposed to never talk about that night ever again, thanks for that, Athos. It was personal and stupid and had nothing to do with the festive terrorism or whatever we're calling this Winterlight business on Paris Satellite."

"You're completely sure of that?" Athos demanded.

"I thought I was, but now you're freaking me out, and I don't know anymore," she hurled back.

Athos nodded, and then disappeared into his own thoughts. Porthos wondered how many times she was going to have to smack him to get him back in the room. "Okay," he said, a few moments later. "Print some coffee, Chevreuse. This is going to be a long night."

She looked furious. "What? I just told you —"

"Her Eminence the Cardinal spent the day establishing the innocence of just about every practicing Elemental residing on Paris Satellite," said Athos in a clipped voice. "I imagine she's going to do the same tomorrow with every Elemental on Lunar Palais. All except for a handful of people with diplomatic immunity, and the one who is above such treatment because he is married to the Regence Royal."

Chevreuse stared back at him. "Oh, hell," she whispered. "So that's it."

"Can those in the room who aren't political analysts maybe explain it for the rest of us?" demanded Porthos, irritated by both of them.

"Buck and her people are being set up," said Athos.

"Or Prince Alek," said Chevreuse. "Or both."

"And if any kind of investigation is raised with the Regence —"

"—it will come to light that some security footage was deleted that night."

"Footage involving the two of them, I assume?" Athos prompted.

"You know I can't answer that." Chevreuse reached out and grabbed his sleeve, dragging him over to the far side of the apartment so that they could converse in rapid, urgent whispers.

Aramis sidled up to Porthos. "It's like they share a brain," she said in a strangled voice.

Porthos nodded. She had been thinking much the same thing. "They're practically finishing each other's sentences, did you notice that?"

Aramis let out a small whimper. "I've spent the last six months dating the girl version of Athos."

Porthos patted her arm sympathetically. "It's okay, baby, it's over now."

Chevreuse's wrist comm trilled. She glanced at it. "This is the secure royal line. Everyone pretend you're not here." She walked over to the window, speaking quietly into her arm.

Athos, Porthos and Aramis' comms all went off at the same time. "You three," said Treville in their ears. "Are you on Lunar Palais?"

"We're off duty," said Athos.

"That is not what I fucking asked."

"Yes, we're visiting Minister Chevreuse at the Palace," said Porthos, stepping in to smooth things over. "What do you need, boss?"

"I need you to get to the Regence right this second, and

stay with her until I get there. There's been an assassination attempt."

"On the Regence?" Porthos gasped, already making for the door.

"On the Cardinal."

When Porthos and the others arrived at the royal chapel, on the ground floor of the Palace, they found that the Red Hammers had already evacuated most of the people attending the Service of Amends, and cordoned off the chapel.

Inside, the Cardinal was propped up against the steps, being attended to by the Regence's personal physician.

The only other people who had been allowed to remain in the chapel, apart from a line of guards and Major Jussac by the doors, were the Regence, Prince Alek, the Duchess of Buckingham, and Mr Linton Gray.

Porthos went immediately to the Regence's side. In a situation like this, a Musketeer's default role was royal bodyguard. Aramis went to Prince Alek, checking in with him quietly.

Athos came in behind them all, having been in conversation with Treville all the way from one end of the Palace to here. "Reports are coming in from all over Paris, your Royal Highness," he announced directly to the Regence. "Eight high-ranked priests of the Church of All were attacked in the middle of an Amends service."

"At the same time?" the Regence asked, her voice crisp and angry. "The same type of attack as on our dear Cardinal?"

Athos nodded. "Each of the victims were encased in a bubble that deprived them of oxygen for between a minute and a minute and a half."

"Breathing the air," said the Duchess of Buckingham in a half-whisper.

"This wasn't an assassination attempt if they all cut out within that timeframe," Chevreuse said, leaning lightly on her cane. "It was a warning. Whoever is doing this, they want us to know they can reach anyone at any time. So what are they working up to?"

"Elementals," the Regence hissed furiously. "This is an insult to us, to all Paris."

"Actually, your highness," corrected Chevreuse. "This is quite obviously a plot to cause further division and distrust between the Church of All and the Elementals. That means we need to look further afield for suspects…"

"Minister Chevreuse is right, of course," said the Cardinal in a croaky voice, pushing her oxygen mask aside. "We must not allow fear to rule us. Today is Amends, the day of forgiveness and reparation."

The Regence was not to be reasoned with. "There is only one religion that brought us to the stars and kept our society together as we built a home here," she declared, sweeping out of the chapel. "It's about time everyone remembered that."

As she followed the Regence out, Porthos caught the devastated look on the face of Alek, the Prince Consort.

"This is going to get worse before it gets better," she muttered to Athos as she passed him.

CHAPTER 6
RESOLUTION
(LEAPING THE FLAMES)

Resolution was the hardest day of Joyeux. When she was younger and first away from home, this was the day when Aramis made a subspace call, no matter what else was going on, to hear the voices of her large, sprawling family, all shouting over each other to tell her how much she was missed.

Now she had been away from home too long, and calling her family was no longer an option. It hurt sometimes, but had become a steady pain deep in her gut, as much a part of her as her arms and legs.

She had Paris. She had a sword and a spaceship. She had Athos and Porthos.

She had the Church of All.

Today of all days, Aramis had the Church of All, and as usual when she was thinking of home, her heart led her to the Luxembourg. Aramis rose early, planning to get to dawn service.

Inside the little church that looked exactly like the one she had first attended as a child, Aramis contemplated the stars and listened to the journeys of the Cosmonauts. The choir raised their voices in song so loud and joyous that she was sure it could be heard from several decks away. In the silence that followed the songs, Aramis whispered her resolutions for the year ahead along with everyone else.

I will love and be loved, I will serve God and the Crown. I shall be a good friend and a good soldier.

This was the craziest Joyeux that Aramis had ever experienced, but there was time for this. For a short while, she allowed herself to contemplate that other life, the one she had always thought she would live.

Perhaps next year.

Aramis rose and left the church. Athos and Porthos waited for her on the steps outside.

"Almost got arrested twice," volunteered Athos.

"I don't know what made them think we were hanging around the Luxembourg for a duel," Porthos added, with a sly smile. "No faith."

Aramis linked her arms in those of her friends. "Come on. We must save Paris, or no one gets to open their presents this year."

"If it is the Cardinal behind this, we can't stop it," said Athos. "We can't fight her, she's too damned powerful."

Aramis frowned. "You really think it's her? Some of these incidents are bordering on sacrilege."

"Whether it's her or not, we're going to have a hell of a diplomatic incident on our hands if the Regence gets any more riled up," said Porthos. "Never mind the Ambassador of Valour – though let's stop and think about the trouble that the Regence could cause by directly insulting

Valour – but at this rate, she's going to say or do something that Prince Alek finds unforgivable."

"Marriage," said Athos in disgust.

"Not for me, thanks, I'm trying to give it up," said
Aramis lightly, and didn't remember until she saw
Porthos' face that her words were tactless. Damn it.

Athos didn't seem to notice. "Today is the day of
Winterlight devoted to leaping the flames," he
volunteered.

Porthos shuddered. "Fire. Fire is worse than snow."

"Leaping the flames is a fertility ritual," Athos
explained. "An ancient form of marriage."

Porthos brightened at that. "Oh, metaphorical flames.
Much better. We can handle metaphorical flames."

Athos' comm chimed and he spoke briefly to Treville
before stepping along faster, towing Porthos and Aramis
both along with him. "The Dead District is on fire," he
reported in a crisp voice. "We need to get there now."

"Metaphorical fire?" Porthos said hopefully.

But no, not with that look on Athos' face. "Actual fire,"
he said grimly.

This time it was Aramis' turn to shudder. Fire on a
space station was everyone's worst nightmare.

The Dead District was the kind of 'living on the fringes of
society' community that always, somehow, managed to
form in the lower levels of every space station and satellite
city in the Solar System, no matter how many times those
in power tried to make sure that they did not.

There was a higher proportion of dirtsiders living here

– tourists whose credit had run out, aliens whose visas had expired, and former planetary residents who had turned to crime or sex work.

Every now and then, the church sent down the Red Hammers or priests or charity workers to clean the damned place out and ship the residents back to their home planets, finding them hospice beds and school place-ments. And then every few months, the Dead District would re-form in a different spot in the maze of vents and tunnels and storage pockets 'beneath' that kept Paris Satel-lite turning.

The current Dead District was close enough to the central power spheres that literally ran Paris Satellite from within that the fire was a major problem. It had been extin-guished by the time Aramis and the others arrived. All available personnel, including Red Hammers and Muske-teers, helped with the evacuation, clearing tunnels so that meditechs could get through to help the wounded and victims of smoke inhalation.

"What's with the masks?" Aramis asked Athos as they passed each other at one point, her carrying a child on her hip towards the nearest first aid station, and him returning from delivering a couple of burns victims to a med station.

Athos tilted his head at her, not sure what she was asking, and Aramis gestured with a wide arm. "Not the oxygen masks. The mask masks."

Many of the civilians had been in costumes, particu-larly the children. The masks were scary faces, but Aramis had noticed something many of them had in common – a repeated motif of water, air, earth, or fire. An Elemental cultural aspect she was missing, she assumed.

Athos looked surprised that she had noticed. Perhaps it

was something he took for granted, from that New Aristo-crat childhood of his that he never spoke about. "It's a wedding thing. Today is one of the days when those who follow the Elemental path pledge their troth to each other, by leaping the flames. It's traditional to have attendants who represent each of the elements. Every dirtside kid, religious or not, knows that if they run around wearing an element mask on the sixth day of Winterlight, their chances of being invited to a ceremony is high."

Aramis was bemused. "And that's something kids want to do?"

"There's usually food," Athos said dryly. "Sweets, that sort of thing."

"Oh." She glanced around, wondering how many of these children had missed out on a meal or at the very least a treat because of the fire. "Are the Church bringing in food supplies for the victims as well as medical assistance?"

"They'd better be."

Several hours later, when things had settled down somewhat, Aramis and Athos found Porthos and the three of them sat down to swig water in a quiet spot near some of the worst of the fire damage.

"Some people go all out with this costume thing," Aramis said at one point. She saw a man standing still on the edge of the crowd, watching the volunteers and services work the area, still dispensing aid to those who needed it.

There was something familiar about him, that man,

though she couldn't see any distinguishing features because he wore a head-to-toe robe of fluttering flames made from brightly coloured fabric.

"Is that what the well-dressed bridegroom is wearing this season?" Aramis asked, meaning it as a joke.

Athos frowned, though, looking the figure up and down. "Perhaps," he said, and there was an uneasiness in his tone that they both responded to.

"What is it?" Porthos asked.

"His sleeves," Athos said. "And – something about the way he stands. I've seen him before. I *know* him."

Aramis glanced across at Porthos, who shrugged.

"Do you know an interesting fact about arsonists?" said Athos slowly. "They almost always return to the scene of the crime. To check out the damage they caused. That man's sleeves look genuinely burnt."

He broke into a run from a standstill. Aramis hesitated only for a moment, and then tore after him. Damn it, no one who drank the way Athos did should be able to move that fast.

The masked man in the fire costume reacted to Athos' approach by darting away. He might have made it, if he didn't have to curve around the crowd to reach an exit.

Athos wasn't close enough to stop him reaching the sphere lift, but the curve of the man's path pulled him back around to where Porthos waited, biding her time. She caught the man in a crash tackle, slamming him to the ground. Athos crashed into them both a few moments later.

"That was fun," said Porthos, not even out of breath. "Let's do it again."

Athos reached out briefly, touching their prisoner's

sleeves. They were indeed charred, smeared with heat damage. "Let's see what you have to say for yourself," he said.

Since Porthos was pinning the man to the ground, and Athos was calling the shots, it was down to Aramis to remove the flame mask so they could get a look at their suspect. She hesitated only a moment before pulling it off.

This wasn't the worst possible face she could have seen under that mask, but it wasn't far off. From the pained look on Athos' face, he agreed with her.

"Linton Gray of Valour," he sighed. "Consider yourself in the custody of the Royal Musketeers."

"I believe that I have diplomatic immunity," replied the Duchess of Buckingham's aide, untroubled by the situation.

"Luckily for us, we can still detain you for your own safety for up to twenty-four hours," said Porthos cheerfully. She bounced slightly on his chest. "I'm betting that if the Duchess of Buckingham knows anything about diplomacy, that immunity of yours is going to mysteriously vanish at some point during that time period." She stood up, stretched and reached a friendly hand down to their suspect. "Come on. Let's be having you."

As Linton Gray rose, Porthos snapped a pair of handcuffs around his wrists. Aramis hadn't even known that Porthos carried cuffs in her regular kit. Arresting people wasn't in their regular duties, though it was well with their power to do so.

"This is bad," said Athos in an undertone, as Porthos gave Gray a shove to start him on his way.

"So bad," Aramis agreed, matching his tone. "But it's

not our problem any more. Merry Joyeux, Athos. We cracked the case."

Athos gave her a look that suggested she was being overly optimistic. "Call your girlfriend, Aramis. This is going to be one hell of a PR job to manage."

"Ex girlfriend," Aramis sighed. But she made the call.

After one of the longest days of Athos' life since he first joined the Musketeers, he was looking forward to the silence of his empty apartment. He only had another day or two before Grimaud would be back from her holiday, and while she was as taciturn as he could ever hope for in an engineer (unless he stole Aramis' android and reprogrammed it to be mute, a possibility he had not entirely ruled out), she still filled the space, and living with her was not the same as living alone.

Actual solitude was a rare thing for him, and Athos prized it above almost all things.

It was 23:00 hours, and he was yet to pour himself a drink. Tomorrow was the final day of Joyeux. There was no more case to be solved, no more festive terrorism plaguing the space station, and he wasn't even on duty.

He could have an early night.

He had only been home for ten minutes or so when he heard the persistent chime of someone leaning hard on his door alert. Athos rolled his eyes, psyching himself up to convince Porthos that he did not need to be fed, and Aramis that he did not need to be hugged or otherwise kept company. No other possibility occurred to him.

Chevreuse stood on his doorstep wearing a plain grey flight suit, her hair back to its natural blonde bob.

Athos blinked, staring at her. "Aramis isn't here," was the first thing he thought to say.

The minister looked exhausted. "I've already spoken to Aramis. I'm here to see you."

"Oh." This made a whole lot of no sense at all, but he stepped back to let her in. "How are things at the Palace?"

"Messy," Chevreuse said, collapsing on his couch and putting her feet up on his coffee table, boots and all. "Irritating. Final."

"I think I'm missing something."

"You need to give me a drink before I tell you more."

Seemed reasonable. Athos fished two bottles out of his cupboard: one wine, and one whiskey. Chevreuse pointed at the wine, and he took the time to find actual glasses. "Linton bloody Gray," he observed as he poured.

"I know," Chevreuse huffed. "I liked him, the bastard."

Athos thought of the almost-flirtation that he wasn't sure had really happened or not, the night of Misrule. "Me too, actually."

She gave him an odd look over the back of the couch. "You hate everyone."

"And yet." He passed her a tolerable glass of red. "How are we on the scale of diplomatic disasters?"

"Maybe a seven out of ten? It hasn't hit the press yet, thank God and All. Our Mr Gray has confessed to the festive terrorism attacks on behalf of a group called the Independent Valour Party. Claims they supplied him with the nano-viruses, all he had to do was set them off on timers across the station. Buck has denied all connection with the group and stripped Gray of the diplomatic protection of her office, but her face is all over the IVP social media accounts. She's their preferred candidate for world leader, so the connection doesn't look good."

Athos raised his eyebrows in mild surprise. "You don't think Buckingham was actually behind it?"

"I don't think she's this stupid. But she doesn't have to be bankrolling the group to be compromised by Gray's actions and his arrest." An uncomfortable look crossed Chevreuse's face. "And then there's the other thing."

Athos had known this was coming. "The deleted security footage."

"It makes it look like I was covering up something political that night," she admitted.

"Well, you kind of were."

Chevreuse gave him a filthy look. "It was two people being careless and impulsive in the wrong bit of corridor, not an interplanetary coup."

"I'm sure the Regence was very understanding about the distinction." Athos paused. "I hate to ask…" He needed to know how badly he was implicated in her disaster.

She gave him a look that made it clear how transparent he was. "No, you're not in trouble. I kept your name out of it."

"Thanks," said Athos. He came to sit on the couch with her. Chev lifted her legs to make room for him, then settled them in his lap. "I'm a little short on job prospects if 'Musketeer' falls through."

Chevreuse patted him on the shoulder. "The position of Ambassador's aide is open. The successful applicant would have to be prepared to spend the rest of the term on Honour, though. Buck is being strategically repositioned far from Paris Satellite, Lunar Palais and the Regence's hot, muscled husband."

"So she's officially innocent of wrongdoing, but still being blamed behind the scenes?"

"Politics," said Chevreuse simply.

Athos leaned in, frowning at her over the top of his wineglass. "What aren't you telling me?"

"It's not a secret," Chevreuse said, sounding fed up. "I've retold it a bunch of times tonight, so forgive me if I drift off during this part. You know the Cardinal's had it in for me for… well, a while."

"Since about five minutes after she met you."

"What can I say, I make an impression." Chevreuse took a long, thoughtful swallow of wine. "The Regence wants to blame someone for this clusterfuck happening under her nose, and the Cardinal has managed to convince her that my loyalties are too closely tied to the Prince Consort, thanks to that piece of footage I made disappear. So – Buck's not the only one being sent into voluntary exile."

Athos hissed at the unfairness of it all. "Seriously?"

Chevreuse pretended she wasn't bothered in the least. "Oh, yes. Paris Satellite and I are done with each other – for now, anyway. The Regence might take me back some time in the future, but I'm not holding my breath." Her arch smile softened. "Don't look so stricken, Athos. I'm not short on resources. Montbazon and I renewed our marriage contract this morning, and I'm off to stay at one of his holdings on Artemisia. I can be a lady of leisure until I find someone willing to let me play politics again."

He fiddled with the clasp on her boot, since it was right there in his lap. "When do you go?"

"Tomorrow."

"So soon?"

"The seventh day of Joyeux is for family, and new beginnings. The sooner I'm out of here, the better. Let someone else deal with the trial of Linton Gray, and Prince Alek's wandering hands. I'm done."

"But," said Athos, still shocked. "But, *fleur-de-lis*."

Her facade cracked. He actually saw her lip wobble. "Shut up. They play Zero-G TeamJoust all over the solar system. I'll find another team. Anyway, we had a perfect season. A perfect, unbeaten fucking season, and no one else has ever done that. Best to quit while I'm ahead, don't you think?" Chevreuse smirked a little, behind her wine-glass. "Packed the trophy in my bags. The Prince will never miss it, right?"

Here was the thing that Athos was blown away by: not that Chev had been screwed over, or even that Cardinal Richelieu had managed to turn a disaster like this into an opportunity to rid herself of a political enemy.

No, the thing that was currently foremost in his head was that he was going to miss Chevreuse.

When had that happened?

He didn't say that, of course. What he said was: "Do you think the Cardinal was behind this whole thing? Behind Linton Gray, and the festive terrorism?"

Chevreuse looked grim. "Let's look at the results. Not me being kicked out, that's gravy on top. But the actual plot resulted in Elementals looking like bad guys, more of a wedge between the Regence and her Elemental husband than ever before, the Duchess of Buckingham losing any chance to gain political mileage out of this visit which has to be a blow to Valour's bid for independence, and oh yes, the Cardinal looks like a hero to everyone because she was attacked at the height of popular sentiment around the Church of All."

"A whole bunch of Joyeux presents for the Cardinal."

"Tied up with ribbon." Chevreuse reached out and took Athos' near-empty glass from him. She placed it carefully on the ground with her own. "I don't want to talk about her Eminence anymore."

"What are you doing?"

She sat there expectantly for a moment, her pale blue eyes fixed on his. "Saying goodbye, idiot."

That was right. She was leaving tomorrow. "Doing the rounds of everyone you know?"

Chevreuse leaned in and punched him lightly on the shoulder. "Just the people I'm going to miss. Montbazon. Aramis. My book club. Alek and Conrad. Our favourite physio, the one with the magic hands and the really good pain pills."

Athos tilted his head in her direction. "I'm a little surprised to find myself on that list."

Chevreuse rolled her eyes at him. "I know most of our socialising has been because of my relationship with Aramis, but you do realise that somewhere along the way you became one of my closest friends?"

Athos blinked. That was – unexpected. "I was not aware."

"You're hopeless. And I will miss you." She nodded towards the wine bottle on the bar. "I'll admit I left you until last because I knew you'd provide the best drinks."

"Oh," he said, and smiled sidelong at her. "Now it all makes sense."

She held out her hand. "A pleasure working with you, Captain Athos."

Athos hesitated only a moment before pulling her into a rough hug, as he had been taught by the two most infuriating people in his life. "Glad to know you, Madame Chevreuse."

"Oh, that sounds terrible," she muttered into his neck. "I'd better get someone else to give me a Ministry position ASAP. What's the government like on Artemisia?"

"Corrupt, probably."

"I like a challenge."

They could have left it at that. They really could. That would have been the sensible thing to do. But Chevreuse was warm in his arms, and this was goodbye, and perhaps it was an overdose of Joyeux sentiment that made Athos turn his face into her cheek.

"Oh," Chevreuse breathed as Athos dragged his mouth down the side of her neck, scratching her lightly with his beard. "That doesn't make things easier."

"No, not at all," he agreed.

"Ten times worse."

"About that, yes."

Her mouth found his, wet and hungry and wanting. There was none of that tentative brush of lips they had almost exchanged on the night of Misrule – this was something else altogether.

Chevreuse was practically in his lap, her hands framing his face, and every time Athos thought about voicing what a bad idea this was, she moved her hips against his, sending waves of heat directly into his veins.

"So," she said finally, her fingers curling into his hair

and her mouth reddened from all the kissing. "What are your resolutions for the new year ahead?"

"I will not make pointless resolutions that I don't intend to keep," said Athos. Sometimes the inevitable was there to be given in to.

"Works for me," she said, and closed her lips around the edge of his ear. "Shall we skip the angst and get straight to the regrettable but extremely hot sex?"

"That's what I love most about you, Chevreuse," Athos drawled. "You're a fucking romantic."

The Joyeux Resolutions of Athos:
I will not sleep with my friend's (recently) ex-girlfriend.
I will not self-sabotage.
I will not blame the wine afterwards.

CHAPTER 7
JOYEUX
(FOR FAMILY)

Porthos awoke to the smell of brandy and green leaves, of coffee and sweet rolls and a strange, plummy flavour to the air that made no sense at all.

Her door slid open for a moment, making the smells more intense. "Your friends are crazy," Bonnie informed her. "There's a cake in the oven, take it out when the timer goes. I'm going to church."

Porthos rose up on her elbows. "Happy Joyeux?" she ventured. She hadn't realised that Bonnie had returned from her family visit, but it was good to have her back.

"Yeah, yeah," muttered Bonnie. "And a jolly new year to you too. Maybe the Joyeux elves will leave you some new friends in your stocking because, have I mentioned? Your current ones are crazy."

"All I want for Joyeux is you," Porthos sang at her.

She could hear voices in the other room, but she took her time about dressing for the day. It might as well be her uniform, since she had a duty shift in the afternoon, but she paired it with a festive wig and some sparkling gold earrings because what was the point of life without making an effort on festive occasions?

"What's all this?" she asked as she stepped out into her living room to be faced with a tree of all things, green and bushy, set in the middle of the floor where her favourite armchair used to be.

It was half-decorated with sparkly baubles, stars and a long, dangling thread of candied popcorn. Porthos blinked, and stared at it.

"The tree is my Joyeux present to you," Aramis called out from somewhere behind the tree. "And my Joyeux present to Athos is choosing to do this here instead of in his apartment."

"Much appreciated," said a grave voice from somewhere near the floor. Porthos looked down and saw Athos bending over the end of the popcorn thread with deep concentration, apparently threading new pieces on with a needle.

"It's a tree," said Porthos, in case neither of them had noticed.

"I've been reading up on Winterlight traditions," said Aramis. "And I thought this was a nice one we could borrow." She ruffled Athos' hair.

"By putting a sparkly tree in my apartment?" Porthos asked, just to be clear.

"Maybe?"

Porthos shrugged. *If you can't beat them, join them.* "Okay, but I'm having cake for breakfast." She was pretty sure that wasn't a Joyeux or a Winterlight tradition, but she was a big believer of making her own. "Also, don't think this gets you out of paying us 50 credits each." She extended her fist to Athos, who bumped it solemnly with his own.

"Of all the mistakes we have made this year, sleeping together was not one of them," he agreed, and then turned his face very quickly back down to the popcorn, as if trying to stop himself volunteering further information.

"So," said Porthos, summoning up as much false cheer as she could. *Fake it until you make it.* "When does the drinking start? Everyone else has been celebrating for days, and we have a week of festive bullshit to catch up on."

"Way ahead of you," said Athos, picking up a glass of red wine from beside him on the floor and saluting her with it.

"There's champagne and cake in the kitchen!" Aramis called behind her as she headed in that general direction. "Bonnie says she will be home later, so this is my only chance to cook for you all."

Porthos and Athos exchanged an alarmed expression.

"Please don't cook anything!" Porthos called after her. "Come put the star on the tree, and we'll print as much food as we need. Nice freshly printed food. Paris Satellite doesn't deserve to be set alight twice in two days."

Aramis hovered at the doorway, frowning reluctantly. "Can I play Joyeux carols if I'm not allowed to cook?"

"God no," said Athos, at the same time that Porthos said:

"If you must."

Aramis' smile lit up the room, and she began to fiddle

with the sound system in the wall. "There will be dancing," she informed them both.

"I hate you all, and also I hate Joyeux," Athos replied, fixing his attention firmly to the popcorn.

Porthos grinned at them both, glad to have them here. "Best Joyeux ever."

Mr Linton Gray lay on the narrow bunk in the solitary cell, deep in the bowels of the Armoury. He was exactly where he needed to be – exactly where he had expected to be, on the final day of Joyeux.

It was restful, after his busy week.

He was not thinking of the Musketeers who had arrested him, or one Musketeer in particular. That could wait. He excelled at many things, but nothing so much as the long game.

Revenge was a slow burn that had lived inside him for a long time. He could wait longer.

The cell door opened, and a woman stepped in. She wore a bright emerald flight suit, though her long fall of shiny black hair suggested she was no pilot. She had a long, prominent scar slashing through one eye.

"I wasn't expecting a roommate," Gray observed.

"Thanks for the offer, but I have much more comfortable lodgings available," she said, dropping on to the foot of his bed as if they were friends. "Brought you a care package from a mutual friend." She tossed a small bag to him.

There were clothes inside, and a clamshell tablet. A

flask of something that smelled festive and a block of expensive chocolate. "Merry Joyeux," he said, not entirely sarcastic. "Isn't she thoughtful, our mutual employer?"

"I'm Ro," said the maybe-not-pilot, holding out a hand. After a moment, Gray held out his own and they shook. "We'll be working together soon, I expect. For the break-out, at the very least."

Gray bit into the chocolate. "When is that scheduled?"

"It will take us a little while to arrange a suitable body before we can stage a convincing death in custody, and Her Indoors would prefer it to be after a decent interval. A couple of weeks, perhaps?"

"I can restrain myself from making my own escape arrangements for a couple of weeks," Gray agreed.

Ro stared at him with undisguised curiosity. "Is it true you can change your face?"

He ran his hands over the distinguished but bland 'Linton' features that he had never grown entirely used to. "Holographic mask. Acquired on the black market. It's bonded to my DNA, so no one's getting it off me unless I'm dead."

"I'll have to remember that if I ever come across your dead body," Ro murmured.

Oh, he liked her. "Want to see?"

Her smile was surprisingly warm. "There are no active cam feeds on this floor for the next hour."

It wasn't a holographic mask. But the excuse had worked so far, for all his previous employers. The Cardinal – and he rather liked the idea of referring to their mutual employer as Her Indoors, he would remember that – had shown no sign that she had any other theories as to how he was able to change his facial features so distinctly.

Gray allowed the 'Linton' face to fall away in favour of the one he used most often. Since he was showing off, he let his hair melt into the shade he had always preferred, the silver-blond that looked so jarring and effective with his youthful face.

"Ohh," breathed Ro, leaning back rather than forward. Interesting reaction. He collected it, as he did every little piece he was learning about her. If they were to work together, he needed to know this woman inside and out. "Good *cheekbones*," she said after a thoughtful moment.

"Thank you," he said politely. "I've put a lot of work into them."

"This is going to make faking your death *so much* easier."

"Obviously."

"What should I call you, once we've killed off Linton Gray?"

He smiled at her, making the most of the charm and handsomeness that belonged to this face.

He had used this face as a weapon since he first insinuated himself among the humans, claiming his first victim. "If we're to be friends, sweetness, you can call me Milord."

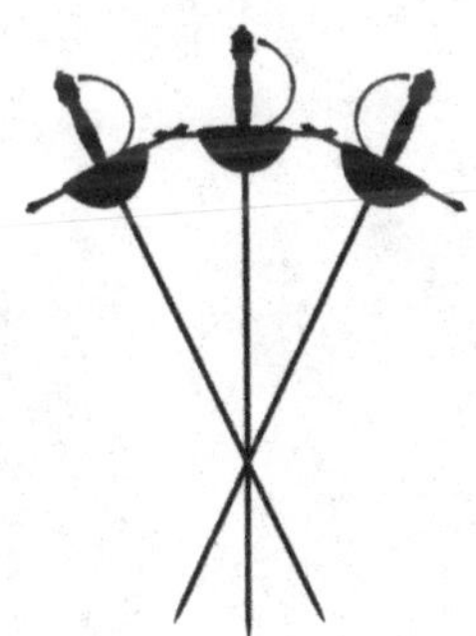

The End... for now.

Follow the story of Porthos, Athos and Aramis when Dana D'Artagnan hits Paris Satellite in *These Valiant Stars* (Musketeer Space #1)

ACKNOWLEDGEMENTS

This story was originally written for my Musketeer Space Patreon backers. Thanks so much for your support!

Thanks to Alexandre Dumas for creating a marvellous adventure and wonderful characters with which I took such extreme liberties.

Thanks also to Katy Shuttleworth for creating this beautiful Musketeers at Joyeux illustration.

ABOUT THE AUTHOR

Tansy Rayner Roberts is an award-winning Australian science fiction and fantasy author who occasionally obsesses about musketeers. She lives with her family in Tasmania.

- Listen to Tansy on Sheep Might Fly, a podcast where she reads aloud her stories as audio serials.
- Read Tansy's stories before anyone else when you pledge to her Patreon: patreon.com/tansyrr
- What tea is Tansy drinking? Find out when you subscribe to her excellent newsletter.

facebook.com/TansyRRoberts
instagram.com/tansyrr

THESE VALIANT STARS

MUSKETEER SPACE #1

Dana D'Artagnan, a brash young spaceship pilot from the outskirts of the Solar System travels to Paris Satellite hoping to join the Royal Fleet. She finds treachery and court intrigue, and makes three great friends, the chaotic and dashing Musketeer pilots Athos, Porthos, and Aramis.

Enemies close in around Dana and her new friends, including the mysterious Agent Ro, the powerful Cardinal Richelieu and the seductive spy Milord.

Only they can save the Solar System. All for one, and one for all!

If you love swordfights, spaceships and snarky LGBTQ+ characters, you'll love this fresh and exciting gender-flipped reimagining of a classic adventure novel. Explore the unforgettable universe of Musketeer Space today.

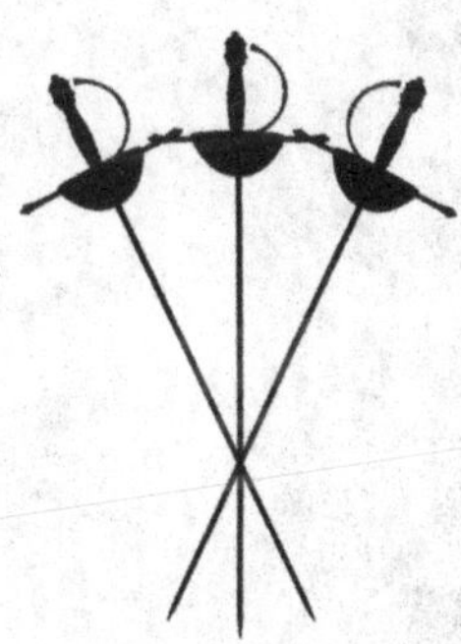

A MIRACLE OF SPACESHIPS

MUSKETEER SPACE #2

When aliens invade, the Royal Fleet rallies to defend the outer planets of the Solar System. Dana D'Artagnan digs deeper into a web of court politics and royal intrigue, desperate to unlock the secrets of a dangerously attractive spy who wears the face of a dead man.

With Athos, Porthos and Aramis fighting on the front line of a space war, Dana will make any sacrifice she can to be at their side and protect the royal family — and the Solar System — from Milord's murderous machinations.

All Dana ever wanted was to be a Musketeer. Now all she wants is to save them.

The thrilling final volume of this epic gender-flipped reimagining of a classic adventure novel. Like the Dumas original, Musketeer Space is funny, sexy, heart-breaking and packed full of swashbuckling chaos-goblins who probably shouldn't be trusted with swords or spaceships.

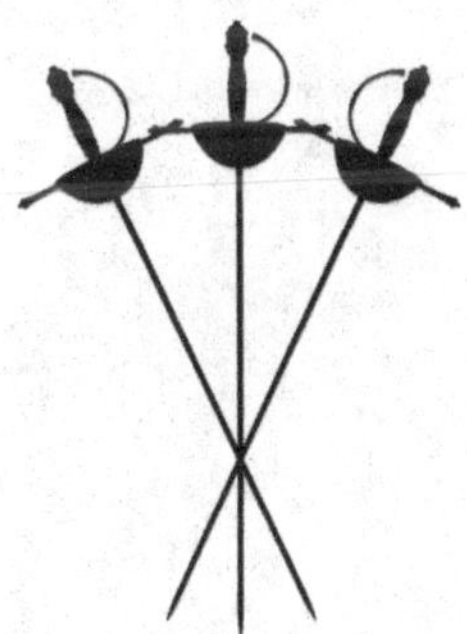

www.ingramcontent.com/pod-product-compliance
Lightning Source LLC
Chambersburg PA
CBHW010343170726
48283CB00009B/2937